To: Roberta & Ronnie

DAISY'S HOPE

for her

JOURNEY

Psalms 118:24

Joan Fields Long

DAISY'S HOPE

for her

JOURNEY

Joan Fields Long

authorHOUSE®

AuthorHouse™
1663 Liberty Drive
Bloomington, IN 47403
www.authorhouse.com
Phone: 1-800-839-8640

Published by AuthorHouse   10/03/2014

ISBN: 978-1-4969-3772-8 (sc)
ISBN: 978-1-4969-3848-0 (e)

Library of Congress Control Number: 2014915873

ABOUT THE BOOK

The author grew up during the Great Depression. Born in 1931, she recalls many of the things that occurred during this period of time and in World War 11. Daisy Pate is a fictional character who is a young widow with four children to rear alone. She has inherited a 300 acre farm in North Carolina from her Grandfather. The story tells of her hope and hard work to keep the farm and her children from being victims of the hard times that all America experienced during what is known as the worst time in our history. Daisy's journey is an account of many disappointments, yet joy, as she helps her children grow into women and men of respect, accountability and into what is now known as "The Greatest Generation". It is the experiences of life on a farm before electricity, telephones, and other conveniences came to rural North Carolina. The setting is a Quaker Community where life revolves around Daisy's home and farm, the church and the public school. Readers of any age will see what life was like in the 1930's and early '40's on a farm.

DEDICATION

My friend, Doris Thornburg, who lives at Little River, S. C. for typing the manuscript.

To Sybil Skakle, for her encouragement. She is part of the Christian Writer's Group of Chapel Hill, N.C. and to the deceased members: Cherry Parker, Frances Bradsher, Libby Love Griffin, Janie Kay Wynne and many others who listened and gave me advice as I read most of the manuscript to them at our meetings. Thanks to my late husband, Cecil Long, my children, Allison Long Morris and Brent Long and his wife Marcie and our grandchildren for their encouragement to publish this book. Most of all, I thank my Lord and Savior, Jesus Christ for giving me the ability to put words on paper.

Sorrow looks back,
Worry looks around,
But faith looks up!
Live simply
Love generously
Care deeply
Speak kindly
Trust in our Creator
Keep Looking up!

Author Unknown

CHAPTER 1

Daisy Pate looked into the smokehouse and sighed, "All the hams and shoulders are gone, only one piece of side meat left. What am I going to cook on Sunday when it's my turn to feed the preacher? I just can't kill one of our six hens or the old rooster as we need the eggs."

It was March 1932 in the time known as The Great Depression. Daisy was a widow on the farm that she had inherited from her grandfather. After the sudden death of her husband, she vowed to rear her four children and not allow them to be placed in an orphanage like some women in her situation. As long as she could pay the taxes nobody would take her home and land.

Closing the smokehouse door, Daisy saw John Henry Smith coming out of the woods behind her barn with a burlap bag in his hand. John Henry was a self-appointed Robin Hood to their community – taking from the haves and giving to the have-nots.

"Here Miz Daisy," John Henry said as he handed her the sack. "I heard tell th' preacher was eatin' with you on Sunday and thought you might could use this."

He ran off before Daisy could even say thank you. She peeped into the sack and there was huddled a big fat Rhode Island Red rooster. She could almost taste the chicken and dumplings that would grace her Sunday dinner table.

She carried the heavy sack over to a chicken coop, opened it and shooed the rooster in and quickly closed the door.

"You stay right there and I'll get you some corn and water. You are a beauty."

On the way back from the well with the water, Daisy stopped and said out loud, "Where in the world would John Henry have gotten a fine rooster like that. I bet he stole it! I can't feed the

1

preacher stolen chicken. It just wouldn't seem right. I'll go ahead and feed and water him. This is Thursday, maybe somebody will come claiming him before Sunday."

She went about her work still wondering what she would put on the table for Preacher Jones, his wife and three finicky daughters.

She talked to herself in the quiet kitchen. "The cressy greens are nice this year. I'll pick some of those and I'll make a molasses cake and maybe some molasses cookies. I've got plenty of flour since the man from the county office came by and brought us some government surplus. It's not very refined, but if I sift it several times and get more of the bran out, it's all right, besides the molasses will make it dark. I have two cans of green beans left from last summer's garden and this would be the perfect time to use them. I'll spare enough of the Irish potatoes that I've saved for seed. It's almost time to plant them. According to the almanac the dark of the moon will be next Friday. I'll open some of my chow-chow, pickles and pear preserves and just maybe they won't notice that I don't have any meat. Besides, Preacher Jones and his wife are both too fat."

Just before time for the children to arrive home from school, a black T-Model Ford chugged up the dirt road leading to Daisy's house. Instead of getting out of the car, the man behind the wheel blew the horn and shouted loudly, "Anybody home?" He spat a stream of brown tobacco juice into the dry grass in the yard.

"It's Abe Johnson, wonder what he wants," thought Daisy as she stepped out onto her front porch.

"Good afternoon, Miz Pate," Abe said, tipping his dirty old hat. "Hope you and your younguns are well."

"Just fine, thank you," Daisy replied politely. "And hope your misses is well."

"She's got the miseries in her hands and feet and can't do much of anythin' now adays." He drawled. "Miz Pate, somebody has been stealin' my Rhode Island Red chickens. You know they're the ones I ordered from the Chatham Nursery. Raised them up from little chicks. They're my pride and joy besides bein' good layers. I think that somebody is that no good chicken thief, John Henry

Smith. He stole my prize rooster, the one I won the blue ribbon for at the county fair."

"Sorry to hear about that, Mr. Johnson. How do you know that John Henry stole them? Maybe a fox has been in your hen house."

"No, ma'am, no sign of a fox carryin' off chickens. But there wuz foot prints of a man's shoe. I was wonderin' if you had seen anythin' of John Henry 'round here. Somebody said they saw him carryin' a tote sack comin' in this direction."

Daisy, not wanting to implicate John Henry, replied, "Mr. Johnson, I believe I have your prize rooster shut up in one of my chicken coops. I fed him some corn and gave him some water. I'll go get him for you."

She returned with the rooster in the same sack in which he had arrived. "If you hadn't claimed him, he might have been fed to the preacher on Sunday."

"Fed to a preacher! Not my prize rooster!"

"Well, if I had the money I'd buy that rooster from you, and cook him for the preacher."

"Nobody's goin' to eat my rooster!" He chugged off in his car slinging rocks and mud.

"Good riddance to you both," Daisy said as she went into the house to wait for her two boys and two girls to get home from school. They had chores to do before the sun went down.

On Saturday, Daisy went to the smokehouse to cut a piece of side meat to cook in her cressy greens and canned green beans. And to her surprise there hung a ham! "I guess John Henry has been here again," she mused. "Come to think of it, one of my hams was missing around Christmas, guess it's been returned to me. The preacher will have meat for dinner after all."

CHAPTER 2

On Monday morning Daisy always did her weekly wash. After the children were off to school, she built a fire under the black wash pot which Adam, her oldest son had filled with clean water from the wooden rain barrel that sat under the eaves of the back porch. Also he had filled some of her wash tubs to be used as her rinse water. She went in the house and brought out all the clothes she could carry. When the water was hot, she carried buckets full and dumped them into a tub where she had shaved off pieces of her homemade lye soap. Then she refilled the wash pot with cold water and added wood to the fire.

Washday was a lot of hard work and many women kept a child home from school to help, but not Daisy Pate. She believed in education. Her children worked when they were home, but never did she keep one out of school when he or she was not sick.

She bent over the washtub scrubbing each piece of laundry on her washboard, being generous with the lye soap. She placed six white sheets in the wash pot and boiled them, poking them into the hot water with a cut-off broom handle. She prided herself on how white her sheets and pillowcases were when hung on the clothesline. After boiling, she placed them in the cold rinse water and lifted them up and down until all the suds were gone and then she wrung all the water out. Her hands turned red from the water and lye soap. Those calloused hands that had blisters in spring from holding a plow handle, blisters in summer from a hoe handle, and blisters in fall from gathering in crops, especially picking cotton, and blisters in winter from an ax handle from chopping wood to keep her family warm.

She enjoyed hanging out clothes especially when a warm breeze gently flapped them to and fro. Also it meant that the hardest part of her job was over.

While doing laundry on Monday morning was a good time for Daisy to think and plan her week's work. It was times like this that she missed her husband. He really had not liked farming but had quit his job in the tobacco factory to move with Daisy and the four young children to her Grandfather's farm. Grandpa Hardin was in poor health and could no longer farm the land that had been handed down in his family ever since the first Hardin had received a land grant from King George of England before the Revolutionary war. Hardins had managed to hang onto the land during the Civil war. They had not been slave owners because they were Quakers. Daisy was the only grandchild as both her parents had died in the flu epidemic in 1918 when she was 20 and her brother was killed in World War I in France. She had lived with her grandparents and had learned farming from both her father and grandfather. She loved the feel of the soil on her hands. The joy that stirred her soul was without description when she saw the first tiny plant peep up out of the ground after seeds were planted.

Grandpa and Grandma had sent her to college after graduation from high school. She had finished her two years at the normal school and received her teaching certificate. Her first and only teaching job was in a city where factories belched black smoke and the coal soot settled on everything. She longed for the fresh air of the farm. However, she met a young man that had a job in one of the factories and they fell in love. She quit teaching school to marry him. They rented a small house outside of town that had a big back yard where Daisy could raise a vegetable garden and keep a cow that her grandparents gave her for a wedding present. Those were happy days. She had the best of both worlds – a husband with a weekly income and a mini farm where she could keep her hands in the soil.

Her husband had been raised on a farm in another part of the state so after Grandma had died and Grandpa was ready to retire from farming he had asked Daisy and Joe and the children to move in with him and take over the farm. Of course Daisy was delighted to return to the land where she had her roots and to be able to rear her children in the same atmosphere she had so loved. Joe had quit his job reluctantly, but could not refuse Daisy the happiness that had come over her the moment she had received her Grandfather's summons. Papers were drawn up making them the sole heirs to the property upon Grandpa's death except an aunt who had a lifetime right to live there until her death. They moved the fall that Adam started to school. Joe and Daisy raised their first crop with the supervision of Grandpa. But by the next winter Grandpa had been continuously growing more feeble and took pneumonia and died the first day of February.

Things went well on the farm for Daisy and Joe for about the first five years. They had good crops and were able to keep their fertilizer and seed bill paid on time and keep the county taxes paid. They even had some money in savings in the bank. But then the depression started, the banks closed and they lost what they had worked so hard to save. Joe became more and more discouraged and wished he had never given up his factory job. He admitted to Daisy that he had never really wanted to be a farmer. Of course she was disappointed to learn this about the man she loved but it never daunted her faith in him as a good husband.

When Franklin Delano Roosevelt became president of the United States, he instigated the "New Deal" and started several government programs that included the CCC camp project. Joe thought it would be a good way to earn some money for his family and to get out from under his obligation to farm.

Sometimes on cold winter nights when Daisy longed for Joe's warm body next to hers, she would have regrets of bringing him to the farm, but then she would remember that many factories had closed and perhaps their situation would have been even worse. At least they could raise their own food on the farm.

After Daisy finished her washing she ate her lunch and went out to the barn to shovel out the manure from the stables that housed the two mules – Maud and Frances. This was not one of her favorite jobs, but somebody had to do it.

She grabbed a pitchfork and walked into the back stable and began to pitch the manure out the window onto the ground. She heard a noise behind her and turning around in the darkest corner of the stable she saw what she thought was a large animal. She was glad she had the pitch fork in her hand, she backed toward the door, but as her eyes became adjusted to the darkness she realized it was not an animal but the form of a man crouched down on his feet.

"Who's there?" she shouted. "Who are you and what are you doing in my barn? Come out where I can see you," she commanded.

"I can't, ma'am," a weak voice replied.

"Why can't you?"

"I'm hurt. My leg is busted."

Daisy could tell by his accent that he wasn't a white man. She suddenly felt panic grabbing at her whole body. She held firmly to the pitchfork and moved a little closer so she could see better.

"Who are you?" she demanded.

"I'm called Bo Little," the weak voice replied.

"How did you hurt your leg?"

"I fell over a dead tree in the woods last night. I saw your barn and came in out of the cold."

Daisy's mind went back to early in the day when she had milked two cows in this barn and Billy Joe, her second boy, had turned out the mules from this very stable. "It's afternoon now. You've been here all that time?"

"Yes, ma'am, I guess I've been passed out. The pain is so bad." He moaned as he spoke.

"Are you running from the law, Bo Little?" Daisy asked.

"Well, not 'xactly, ma'am."

"Not exactly, what do you mean by that?"

"I was workin' for a white man over in Mullins County."

Daisy remembered that Mullins County was known as bootleg whiskey paradise. "And just what kind of work were you helping him do?"

"I reckon I was helpin' him make likker," he replied with hesitation in his voice. He got mad at me after he'd drunk some of his own makins' and he began to beat me with a big stick and I commenced to runnin' and 'bout that time I saw the Sheriff's car comin' down the road and I ran off in the woods and laid low and I heard the Sheriff fire his gun and I don't know what went on back at that still, but I started runnin' agin and I ended up way over here in the dark, and that's when I busted my leg. I shor' am thirsty and hungry, ma'am. I'm skairt to go back to Mullins County. They may think I worked for him and might sic the Sheriff on me for helpin' him."

Daisy thought to herself, "Well, what am I supposed to do with you? You'll have to come out in the light where I can see that leg. See if you can crawl."

Bo scooted and dragged himself out into the barnyard.

Daisy still held the pitchfork in one hand as she got up close enough to see his leg. His right foot was swollen over the top of the old worn out shoe.

"Pull that shoe off and let me take a look." He pulled off the shoes and pulled up his worn faded dirty denim overalls leg. His leg was cut and scratched. Dried red blood was caked on his dark skin mixed with dried mud.

"You stay right here while I get some water and rags."

She ran toward the house still carrying the pitchfork. She grabbed a pan of water, some clean rags and a bottle of Watkins liniment.

Never before in her thirty-two years had she ever touched a colored man's leg. She had been touched by a colored woman who had helped out when her babies were born but this was a new experience. She gently washed the wounds on his leg. Some began to bleed again as the rag touched them. His blood was bright red like hers, which in a way surprised Daisy. "I believe your ankle is badly sprained." He winched as she touched this swollen ankle. "I'm going to rub some of this liniment on it and wrap it tightly with this piece of cloth. I used to see the doctors do that to athletes who got hurt while playing when I was in college. Just sit here in the shade while I get you some food."

Daisy came back with two big cold biscuits with ham from the Sunday dinner, a piece of her molasses cake and a tall glass of milk.

"Now eat this and see if you don't feel better."

Daisy looked at the young black man as he quickly ate the food. He was tall and slender with a broad nose and white even teeth.

"How old are you, Bo?"

"I reckon I'm 'bout 22. My mammy's dead and I don't think nobody wrote it down when I was born. Where's yo' man, he won't shoot me for bein' in y'all's barn, will he?"

"No, Bo, there's no danger of that. My name is Mrs. Pate, Daisy Pate. I have four children who'll be coming home from school soon."

"This sure is good food, ma'am. Thank you. I'll be on my way soon's I can walk a little. Yo' sure is kind to me."

"Where will you go?"

"I dunno, ma'am."

"My Grandpa used to have a man that helped him on the farm here some and he'd sleep out in a little room that Grandpa built beside the shed where we keep our truck. My girls use it for a playhouse now, but maybe we could fix you a bed in there and you could stay the night. Just stay here until my boys get home from school and they can help me move you."

When the children came in from school, Daisy told them about the colored man she had found in the barn.

"Mother, weren't you scared to death?" eight-year-old Mary Lou asked her mother. "I've heard that colored men are mean and we aren't to get near them. That's what my friend Carrie said her mother told her."

"Well, I was startled when I first saw him. But he is very nice and needs our help. He can't walk on his sprained ankle. I was wondering if we could fix up the playhouse where Mr. Hill used to sleep and make him a bed in there."

All four children and Daisy went to the barn to see this stranger.

"We've decided you can stay," Daisy told Bo. "We've brought a tree limb that you can use for a walking stick and we'll help you get up to the car shed."

Reluctantly the boys helped Bo to his feet. With Adam's help he walked to the shed and sat down on an old chair. Bo's smile and words of appreciation soon made the children feel at ease.

"We all have chores to do," Daisy told Bo. "We'll get you some quilts and a pillow and bring you some supper after while."

"Wish I could help you with them chores, ma'am."

That night after supper and homework Adam came into his mother's bedroom. "Mother, I hope we aren't doing the wrong thing by letting Bo stay here. You know how folks around here feel about Negroes."

"I know, Adam. I was just thinking what would Grandpa have done in this situation, and I know he would have taken care of him or anyone else that needed a place to sleep or food."

Daisy slept rather restlessly that night. She dreamed of colored people dancing around a fire in some sort of jungle that was filled with trees that had faces of white people painted on them.

CHAPTER 3

Before the children left for school, they had all stopped in to see how Bo was feeling. His leg was still swollen, but his appetite was good when Daisy brought him some breakfast.

"Yo' shor' is good to me, Miz Pate. I 'preciates all you've done for me, but I should be goin' 'long an' not bother yo' any more," Bo drawled.

"I don't believe that leg is healed enough for you to walk on it just yet, Bo. Take it easy here today and we'll see how you're doing tomorrow," Daisy replied.

"Is there anything I could help you do today while I'm jus' settin' here?" Bo asked.

"Well, I guess you could shell some corn for the chickens. I'll get you some from the crib."

She hurried to get a basket of corn and a bucket to put it in.

"We used to have a corn sheller, you know one of them that you put the corn in and turn a handle, but the handle came off and I don't know how to fix it."

"I'm handy at fixin' things, Miz Pate. Soon as I gits on my feet I'll see if'n I can fix it."

"That would be nice, Bo. Since my husband is gone, I've had to let a lot of things go because I don't know how to fix them or have the time either. A farm this size needs a lot of hands to keep it going. The handle on my grinding stone has come off, also. My ax is so dull I can hardly chop wood."

"A nice lady like yo'self ought not to have to chop wood and work so al' fired hard, Miz Pate."

"Well, if I don't do it, whose goin' to?" she replied. "I aim to keep this farm and keep my children together and all of us from starving to death."

11

"I b'lieve yo' could use a hired hand."

"Bo, the way things are going these days with the depression and all, I don't think I could afford one. I do some trading of work with our neighbor – Mr. Sonner. He's German and was born and raised over there, but came here when he was a young man and hired himself out to Mr. Winston Berrier. When Mr. Berrier died leaving no heirs he willed his farm to Mr. Sonner. Mr. Sonner had married one of the girls from here in the community and they have made a real go of the farm. He says I can turn off work good as any man," Daisy said proudly.

Daisy went to the barn to finish cleaning out the stables. The manure would be good to spread on the fields and be turned under when she plowed them, getting them ready for planting cotton and corn, her two main money crops. The wheat and oats she had planted in the fall were growing good. She had a feeling that this year's crops would do well.

She thought about what Bo had said about a hired hand. She wondered if he was asking for the job.

She went to the house at noon to check on the fire in the wood stove and to see if the pinto beans she was boiling were done. They were done so she fixed a plate with a hunk of cold cornbread and a glass of milk and took them out to Bo.

She returned to the house and was fixing herself a plate when the Sheriff's car drove up.

Thomas Ferrell had been elected sheriff for his second term. He had gone to school with Daisy and had been her friend from first grade.

"What brings you out this way, Thomas?" Daisy asked, after they had exchanged greetings.

"Well, the Sheriff in Mullins County sent word to me that a nigger by the name of Bo Little had been helpin' a man make likker and when they busted up the still the nigger had run off. My little girl, Carrie, got sick at school this morning and while I was driving her home, she said that your daughter Mary Lou told her that a colored man with a hurt leg was staying with you all."

Daisy sighed and looked Thomas straight in the eye and said, "Thomas, I won't lie to you, I found this man hurt and hungry in my barn yesterday afternoon. I fixed up his leg, fed him and gave him a place for the night. What's wrong with that? Don't you remember the story of the good Samaritan that we learned in Sunday School when we were children?"

"Of course I remember that story. And I didn't say anythin' was wrong about helpin' somebody out. But you know it's dangerous for you as a widow woman to be out here on this farm all alone with a nigger man. It just ain't right."

"I'm not afraid of him," Daisy replied. "He's been shelling corn for me this morning and when he is better he is going to do some repairs for me. I'm thinking of hiring him on as a hand to help me with the crops this year."

"Well, I would hope you wouldn't do that," Thomas replied. "Since he wasn't caught workin' at the still I can't take him in. But I was worried about you bein' here alone with him."

"Stop worrying. Bo isn't going to hurt me. He can't walk much."

"Maybe I'd better talk to him anyway," Thomas said. "Where is he?"

"Out in the lean-to beside the car shed."

Daisy went out with him. They stepped into the lean-to, but no one was there.

"He must have seen your car, got scared and ran off. Bad as his leg is I don't know how he could walk. It will probably get infected and be worse than it is."

"Don't worry about him, Daisy. He's probably plenty tough. I'll go along now but if you need me send for me."

"Thanks, Thomas, but I'm not the least bit concerned about Bo Little hurting me."

After he had gone, Daisy began calling Bo's name.

"I'm in the outhouse, Miz Pate. I wuz afraid the sheriff had come to get me." He opened the door and hobbled back to the lean-to.

Daisy could see fresh blood coming through the piece of sheet that she had used as a bandage on his leg. "Here, let me take a look at that leg." She unwrapped the bandage. "That cut looks worse. Let me get some more liniment and a clean bandage."

She fixed it, told him to lie down and prop his leg up.

"Thank ya', Miz Pate. Why are you so good to me?"

Daisy went back to her job, cleaning out the stables. The smell was almost more than she could stand. "Maybe I should hire Bo. I'll talk to the children about it. We couldn't pay him much."

CHAPTER 4

The next morning when Daisy took Bo his breakfast she found him moaning and thrashing about on his makeshift bed.

She called his name, but nothing coherent came out of his mouth. She leaned down and touched his forehead. It was hot with fever.

"I'll have to get him to a doctor. His leg must be infected. He might get gangrene," she told the boys before they left for school. "You'll have to help me get him into the back of the truck." She backed the truck as close to the door of the lean-to as possible. The three of them rolled him onto a quilt an after much struggling lifted him onto the truck. They put a pillow under his head and covered him with another quilt.

"Wish I could go with you, Mother," Adam said.

"No, you go along to school with the others. The cows have been milked and put out to pasture, so have the mules. I'll feed the chickens and pigs when I get back."

She drove the old Ford pickup truck as fast and as carefully as she could over the rutty dirt roads. Half an hour later she stopped in front of Dr. Foxx's white frame colonial style house. She knocked on the front door and Mrs. Foxx opened it.

"Why, Daisy Pate, what brings you here so early in the morning, is one of your children sick?"

"No, ma'am." Is Dr. Foxx here?"

"Yes, but he's having his breakfast." What is the problem?"

"Mrs. Foxx, I have a colored man in my truck who has a badly infected leg."

"A colored man! What in he world! Why did you bring him here? The colored doctor is at the county seat, you should take him there."

"But there isn't time. He has a high fever and is delirious."

Dr. Foxx stepped into the hallway. "What is it, dear?"

"It's Daisy Pate and she has a colored man with her that's sick. I'm trying to get her to take him to the colored doctor in town."

Dr. Foxx was a gray-haired kindly man who had brought Daisy into the world and had credit for birthing at least half the babies in the county who had been born since the turn of the century.

"Hello, Daisy, what's going on?" he asked.

Daisy explained the situation.

"I'll get my bag and come out to the truck," he replied in a calm voice.

"Get your coat, Samuel. It's too cool to be outside without one," his wife reminded.

Dr. Foxx returned with his coat, hat and bag. He looked into the back of the truck. Daisy let the tailgate down and Dr. Foxx climbed into the truck.

He examined Bo's leg, felt his pulse and his forehead.

"Who is this boy?" he asked.

"His name is Bo Little and I found him in my barn a couple of days ago. I bandaged his leg and I've been feeding him and trying to keep him off of it. I think it's gotten infected."

"You are mighty right it is infected. There's not a lot I can do for him. He needs to be in the hospital."

"But will the hospital take a colored man?" Daisy asked.

"Yes, they have a ward for the colored. I'll follow you on over there and make sure they take him."

"He doesn't have any money, Dr. Foxx, and neither have I just now. When I sell my crop in the fall I'll have some," Daisy said.

"Don't worry, Daisy. I'm sure they will let you sign a note for him. You certainly are a kind person to be so concerned about a colored man."

Dr. Foxx went back to the door and told his wife he would be back in about an hour.

Daisy drove into the county seat and straight to the hospital. It had been built with nickels and dimes from the community where people had banned together to raise money and had contributed both time and work into building a place to care for their sick. She drove around to the back to the door marked "colored entrance."

Dr. Foxx went in and quickly two big black men came out with a stretcher and carried tall skinny Bo into the hospital.

Daisy parked the truck and went in the same door that Bo had gone through. She was met by a black woman in a starched white uniform.

"May I help you?" the woman asked in an accent that Daisy knew was not Southern.

"Yes. I brought Bo Little here. I was wondering what you are going to do with him."

"You must be Mrs. Pate. Dr. Foxx said you would be responsible for the patient. Would you please step this way and fill out these papers, please." She emphasized the word please.

"I'll fill them out, but I won't have any money until fall, she replied."

"Is the patient one of your servants?"

"Oh, no! I hardly know him. I do plan to hire him to work on my farm."

"Well, you can take the bill out of his wages," she said curtly.

"Yes, I guess I can," Daisy replied.

After filling out the papers she sat down and waited. Dr. Foxx came out in a few minutes and told her that the colored doctor was treating Bo. They were trying to get the fever down and were working on the infection in his leg.

"You go on back home and come back in two days and perhaps he'll be well enough to go home with you. You did the right thing, Daisy, by bringing him for help. If more people had compassion like you this world would be a better place."

"Thank you, Dr. Foxx. I'll be getting on home. I have a lot of work to do."

As she drove home, she was thinking about Bo and hoping that when he awakened in this strange place that he would not be scared and try to run away.

CHAPTER 5

Daisy arrived home and went straight to her work. "I'm glad I'm healthy and strong," thought Daisy. "I really do need help. It won't be long until school's out and the children will be here to help. That Adam, he's only 14, but he can work like a man. Now Billy Joe, he'd rather play baseball than work, but he's a good youngun' and I have to let him have time to play and be a child. It's not fair when younguns' have to grow up too soon. Oh! Joe, why did you have to die and leave me?"

She pushed a strand of blond hair that had come loose from the ball at the back of her neck. "I think I'll have my hair bobbed off like a lot of women are wearing theirs these days. It would be so much easier to take care of and cooler, too. I wonder what Preacher Jones would think if I came into church next Sunday with my hair cut short."

It was 1:00 o'clock when Daisy came in the house to eat her lunch. "Think I'll go to the mailbox before I eat. I might get some more seed catalogs. 'Bout all that I ever get anymore."

She reached in the dilapidated mailbox. "Another one of those things that needs fixing around here," she sighed. To her surprise she pulled out a letter addressed to her. The envelope was pink and the handwriting was very neat. She turned it over and on the back was the return address – Miss Lillie Fern Hardin Apt.1305, Magnolia St., Washington, D.C.

"A letter from Aunt Lillie Fern," she said out loud. She sat down on the ground beside the mailbox and read the letter.

Dear Daisy and Family,

It's been a long time since I've written. I was very sorry to learn of the death of your husband. But we all know that God knows best.

I've decided to retire from my position as private secretary to Senator Calhoun. I'm getting on in years and I must make plans for my future. I don't think I'd like to spend the remainder of my life in this big city. I've been thinking a lot about home, remembering my childhood and thinking about Papa and Mama. I think when I die I'd like to be buried beside them in the cemetery there by the church. I was wondering if you would allow me to come live with you there in the house where I grew up. I am still in good health and I could help you with the housework and cooking. I never was a field hand even when I was young, so I wouldn't be much help to you there, but I could earn my keep in other ways. I've saved a little money over the years and I have a small pension every month and I'd be able to contribute to your household expenses.

You think about it, and if you decide you want me to come, write back and let me know. I'm planning to retire on my birthday, May 23rd.

With Love,
Your Aunt Lillie Fern

P.S. I have some furniture that I could bring along, a mahogany bedroom suite, a cedar chest, living room furniture, victrolla, a sewing machine and, of course, my piano.

Daisy jumped up and let out a yell, "Aunt Lillie Fern, you are an answer to prayer. I need all the help I can get!"

She skipped like a child back to the house. "Oh! But I must talk this over with the children. How are they going to feel about an older person living in the house with them? And does Aunt Lillie Fern know what it will be like to live in the house with four lively children!"

When the children came home from school, Daisy read Aunt Lillie Fern's letter to them. The girls were excited, remembering birthday cards with a quarter taped in them, and a big box of presents that arrived by mail every Christmas from Great Aunt Lillie Fern. Neither Elizabeth nor Mary Lou could remember ever having seen her, but they knew who she was in the picture of Great Grandpa and Great Grandma and their family that hung on the wall in the parlor.

Adam and Billy Joe were not quite as excited as the girls.

"Another female in this house," Billy Joe said, "and I bet she doesn't like baseball or know anything about it."

She's a wonderful cook," Daisy said. "While we're in the fields working, she'll be cooking our dinner and when we come in it will be ready for us to eat!"

"That sounds good to me," Adam declared. "I'm always so hungry after working hard and I hate to wait for Mama to cook."

"Then does this mean that you all agree that Aunt Lillie Fern should come to live with us?"

Each head nodded yes.

"It will take some getting used to for all of us. But I'm sure if we all cooperate it will work out for the good of all of us. I'll write her a letter tonight."

"How will she get here, and who will bring her furniture?" Elizabeth asked.

"I'm sure she will come on the train and she will have her furniture shipped by rail. We'll have to go meet her at the station."

In their excitement over Great Aunt Lillie Fern they had forgotten about Bo.

"What happened to Bo?" Adam asked.

"His leg is infected and he is in the hospital," Daisy replied.

"Will the doctor have to cut his leg off?" Elizabeth asked.

"No, I don't think so. They wanted to keep him for a couple of days. I have to go back to get him later in the week. What do you all think about our hiring Bo to help us with the crops? Perhaps he could fix up the old tenant house that Grandpa used to have a family living in. It hasn't been used in years but he seems handy with tools and he can do any repair it would need."

"I think it's a good idea," Billy Joe replied. "With him here to help work, I could have more time to play baseball."

"With Bo and Great Aunt Lillie Fern both coming to live here, our family is getting bigger and bigger," Elizabeth said. Counting on her fingers, she decided it would be seven people.

CHAPTER 6

The great depression raged on especially for farmers in North Carolina. Daisy Pate tried hard to keep from becoming depressed over her financial situation. Christmas was coming and her four children were looking in the catalogs that came in the mail and making their wish list.

Aunt Lillie Fern was a bright spot for Daisy. Her pleasant personality and her knowledge of making do with whatever was on hand whether it was food, clothing, or as a peace maker when the children got into quarrels, helped Daisy. Lillie Fern played her piano and they would all gather around and sing, especially on Sunday afternoons. Sunday was the one day that they built a fire in the fireplace in the parlor. She gave the girls piano lessons and it wasn't long until they were anxious to go into the parlor even when it was cold to practice.

The children drew names at school and that meant four presents to buy; Daisy's cash money was low as she had been saving to pay the taxes on the farm that were due the end of December. Also, the license plates on the truck would have to be renewed on January 1st or she would have to park it.

The girls were especially concerned about their gifts for the names they had drawn at school. Lizzy had the name of whom she believed to be the most stuck up girl in her class, Grace Callahan.

"Mother, Grace has the nicest clothes of anyone in our whole school. She has a beautiful new red coat that has a black velvet collar and a black velvet muff that hangs around her neck. Their chauffeur drives her to school everyday in a big car. Oh! Why did I have to draw her name?"

"Don't worry, honey, we'll think of something."

Aunt Lillie Fern spoke, "Honey, before I left Washington I bought a whole lot of things at an Efird's store that was going out of business. I have a drawer full of things that any girl would be pleased to receive."

"Did you say Efird's Store?"

"Yes."

"That's the store where Grace said her mother bought her new coat in Raleigh."

"Mary Lou, how about you? Whose name did you draw?" Aunt Lillie Fern asked.

I got a boy's name. John Ingram. He's the poorest boy in our class. His Mother died about two years ago and his clothes are always dirty and he doesn't smell good."

"Poor little fellow. Sounds like he could use a nice gift. I bought some things for boys, too. Let's go take a look and see what we can find. You come along, too, Daisy. We'll need your advice."

To the girls it was like shopping in a real department store to see all the things in Aunt Lillie Fern's bureau drawers. Lizzy selected a Shirley Temple bracelet. It was a replica of one she had worn in a movie. It was even in an Efird's box. Mary Lou found a warm pair of gloves and a matching scarf for John Ingram.

"We'll have to see what the boys will need for the names they drew," said Aunt Lillie Fern. "There's probably something here they can use."

"Aunt Lillie Fern, you are a God-send," Daisy said, giving her a hug.

The school had a Christmas program on the last day before Christmas vacation. Each of the children had a part. Parents were invited. Daisy took an afternoon off from plowing under the cotton stalks. The old tractor had given her some trouble, but Bo had worked on it and although it was noisy and slow, she was managing to get the winter plowing done. The red earth smelled good to Daisy as the turning plow dove deep beneath the dry cotton stalks and rolled over like waves on the ocean.

Aunt Lillie Fern went with Daisy to the schoolhouse. There was a big decorated tree in the auditorium. The decorations had been made by the lower grade children – multicolored chains made of construction paper, popcorn strung meticulously together with red berries from Chinaberry bushes which were not berries at all, but the seeds that formed in the fall, made bright strands wound around the cedar tree that some of the older boys had cut from the woods that were part of the school property. The fragrances of pine made into wreaths with bright red bows decorated the back of the stage and mingled with the cedar tree gave an air of Christmas to the plain room filled with excited children.

In a rural community the school and the churches were the gathering places for entertainment as well as educational and spiritual enrichment. All the parents knew each other, their children, the teachers and the principal.

Lillie Fern was glad to see so many people that were grand children of the ones with whom she had gone to school. It was no longer a two-room wooden frame building but was a nice brick building with a gym that was attached at one end and used as an auditorium. Many of the people did not know that Lillie Fern had returned from Washington, not for a visit this time, but to be a permanent resident at this home of her youth.

The principal, Mr. White, greeted everyone and turned the program over to Miss Tesh, the music teacher, who also taught art. Miss Tesh had one of the senior class girls to play the piano and she led the audience in several Christmas carols before each grade put on their program. Daisy and Lillie Fern were so proud of the parts that the Pate children played.

"Your children are so smart," Lillie Fern, whispered to Daisy. Daisy shook her head yes!

After the program, the gifts under the Christmas tree were given out. Each child received a gift. Principal White and the teachers had made sure that no one was left out.

Lillie Fern had made a batch of her special recipe of sea foam candy and fixed a package for Principal White and each teacher.

The Pate children walked home with Daisy and Lillie Fern. They were excited over the gifts they had received. Adam had a box of firecrackers.

"I'll save these until Christmas morning, then I'll pop them," he said.

"You will be careful, won't you?" Daisy asked.

"Oh! Mother! You know I will." Billy Joe had a bag of marbles. He was already the best marble shooter in his class. Elizabeth had four different colors of hair barrettes. Mary Lou received a box of store-bought chocolate candy. Their teachers had given each child two pencils along with a candy bar.

Mary Lou said, "Our next exciting day will be our Church Christmas program and then it will be Christmas! Mother, when can we go to town shopping?"

Elizabeth spoke up, "And when are we going to put up our Christmas tree?"

"We have to go out in the woods and find one," Daisy replied.

"I know where there is a pretty one, in the woods behind the barn," Adam said.

"We'll have to check it out. Perhaps Sunday afternoon will be a good time. I think tomorrow we'll go to town. But remember, children, we don't have a lot of money to spend this year."

"I've been saving up all year," Adam said.

"So have I," Billy Joe echoed.

After the chores were done and supper was over, the children went to bed.

"Aunt Lillie Fern, I'm really concerned about what I'll get the children this year. Adam wants a bicycle so badly. There isn't any way that I can afford one."

"Maybe he will win one," Little Fern replied.

"Win one, what do you mean?"

"He entered a contest, one that was sponsored by the Future Farmers of America. He wrote an essay on why he wanted to become a farmer. I helped with his grammar and punctuation and typed it on my old Underwood. I have a feeling he will win. First prize is a bicycle and second is $25.00."

"Wouldn't that be an answer to prayer? But it's getting mighty close to Christmas and he hasn't heard anything. Besides I'm sure thousands of boys entered the contest."

"Think positively, Daisy."

"Billy Joe wants a new baseball glove. His old one is a hand-me-down and it is just about worn out. He loves baseball so much. I wish I could get him a real pair of shoes with cleats. Elizabeth wants clothes, especially the pretty sweaters she has seen in the catalogs. And, of course, Mary Lou wants a Shirley Temple doll."

Lillie Fern was thoughtful for a moment and then spoke up in her soft but firm voice, "Daisy, I've been thinking, you and the children have welcomed me into your home so graciously."

"But Aunt Lillie Fern, this is where you belong. Grandpa left you a lifetime right to this house and farm."

"I know, but having an older person move in isn't always the easiest thing on a family."

"It's wonderful having you here. You are so much company to me and the children love you and you take such a load off me doing so much cooking and housekeeping."

"I am happy here, and that's why I want to help you pay the taxes. You said you had saved up enough for the taxes. Why not use that money for the children's Christmas and I'll pay the taxes."

"You're too generous. You've worked hard all these years to put away money for your old age. I can't let you spend it on us."

"You and your children are my security. Without you all I'd still be living alone in a dingy apartment in Washington."

"I'll let you do it this year, but by next year hopefully the economy will be better. Sometimes I feel like givin' up on farming and goin' back to teaching school. Only thing, I'd have to get some more teachers' training and that would cost more than I could afford."

"Well, let's go to bed, Daisy. We should get an early start to town tomorrow as I need to go to the bank and go by the courthouse and pay the taxes."

Everyone was up early and chores got done quickly. Bo, who now had the old tenant house fixed up enough to sleep in came by for his breakfast.

"We're going to town, Bo. Do you think you'll be able to get that cotton field finished plowing under today?"

"Yes, ma'am, if that ol' tractor holds together. I wish Santie Clause would bring you a new 'un."

"I wish he would, too, Bo. Can we get you anything from town?"

"Yes'um. Could you git me a pretty box o' candy? One dats fix up nice?"

"I think we can do that. You getting it for your girl friend?" Daisy teased.

"Yes'um. I hopes I can go home for a day or so at Christmas 'ifen yo' can spare me."

"We can manage that. But do you think it's safe for you to go back to that county you escaped from?"

"Miz Lillie's been writin' letters to her for me and she stayin' at her Aunt Bertie's house over in Montgomery County. She got a job teaching school. So I plans to go to her Aunt's house. Some o' my folks lives near there. My Ma's daid and my Pa run off up North a long time ago and we ain't heard from him in years – reckon he's daid, too."

"How are you going to get there?" Daisy asked.

"I reckon I'll walk."

"That's at least 25 miles."

"I's walked furder than dat."

"Do you know how to ride a mule?"

"Shore I do."

"Well, what if you rode one of the mules?"

"Which one?"

"Kate, of course. Ol' Maud wouldn't let nobody get on her back. The children have all rode Kate."

"That sho' be nice of yo', Miz Daisy. But what if'n dat mule runs away while I's dar?"

"She won't if you put her in somebody's barn. You can take a along some corn to feed her."

"That would be just like the Christmas story of Mary and Joseph," Mary Lou spoke up. "Mary rode on a donkey which is like a little mule all the way from Nazareth to Bethlehem where baby Jesus was born in a stable."

"I knows that story. My Mama use ter tell it to us younguns' every Christmas."

"Here, Miz Daisy, is the money ter buy the candy with and there's enough to get some good smellin' fume and here, children, I'm gonna give each of you a quarter to spen' jus' like yo' wants to when you goes ter town."

"Bo, you shouldn't do that. I haven't been able to pay you much of anything since you've been here."

"Yo' gives me room and board and yo' all so kind ter me. I's been hirin' out ter Mr. Frazier when yo' didn't need me and I been savin' what he pay me ter pick cotton."

Each child thanked Bo, and his white teeth showed and his thick lips parted into a big smile.

Everyone was ready to go by 9:00. It was a frosty morning. The boys covered up with a quilt in the back of the truck while the women folk sat in the cab. They also covered with a quilt as it was before heaters were installed on trucks. This was not a trip to the nearest village but a trip to the county seat, a city with many tall buildings and stores and streetcars that ran on tracks in the middle of the street.

Daisy found a parking place right away. The boys wanted to go off alone to do their shopping. The girls went with Aunt Lillie Fern and Daisy went alone so she could buy gifts for the children. Everyone met back at the truck at noon. They went into a nearby park and ate the ham biscuits and cake that Daisy had packed. She had bought each of them a 'Cocola' in a nearby store.

"Anyone getting tired?" Daisy asked.

"Only my feet," said Aunt Lillie Fern." You know I had almost forgotten what it's like to walk on cement streets."

"Will everybody be done about 2:00?" Daisy asked.

Lillie Fern said, "There's a good movie showing at the Centre Theater. Would you mind if I took the children to see it? It might be about 2:30 when it's over. You can come with us Daisy."

"A movie!" Mary Lou jumped up and down with excitement. "I've never been to a movie."

"Well, it's time you got to go to one. I used to go all the time in Washington."

"I'll keep on shopping," Daisy replied. "You children behave and mind Aunt Lillie Fern and be sure to thank her."

"We will," they echoed.

Daisy sat a little longer on the park bench. The crisp December air felt good. The smells of the city, the smoke from factory stacks mingled with the gasoline and oil odors from the cars and trucks made her glad that she lived in the country where the air was fresh and clean. "I suppose my children are missing some of the things the city has to offer like movies, the library and museums, but the farm offers a better place to rear children, especially since I'm a widow," she mused to herself.

They arrived home excited about their day in town. Each child had their own hiding place for the gifts they had bought each other, their Aunt and Mother. The next day Lillie Fern went to the mailbox and there was a letter from the Headquarters of the Future Farmers of America. It was addressed to Mr. Adam Pate. She held it up in front of her eyes. My! How I would like to open this, but it would be unfair to Adam. I'll let him be the first to open it.

It was lunchtime and as all the family was gathered at the kitchen table Aunt Lillie Fern said, "By the way, Adam, a letter came for you today from the Headquarters of the Future Farmers of America."

"What, a letter, where is it?" Adam said excitedly.

"Look under your plate," she replied.

His fingers could hardly open it. He pulled it out and read it out loud.

Dear Mr. Pate,

 We wish to congratulate you on your excellent essay on "Why I Would Like to Become a Farmer." Out of the some 3,000 entries, our panel of judges decided yours was best. As you know, first prize is a boy's bicycle. You have won and it is being shipped to you by freight and should arrive before Christmas. Congratulations! Your picture and essay will appear in our next publication. Please fill out the enclosed receipt when the bicycle arrives, so we can complete our records. Sincere thanks for your interest in becoming a farmer and keep up the good work.

Sincerely,
Board of Directors, etc.

Adam was jumping up and down with excitement, so were the other children. Daisy and Lillie Fern looked at one another with big tears of thanksgiving running down their faces.

"I wish we had the telephones like we had when we were children and we could call the freight office," said Lillie Fern. Papa always kept up those phone lines. It does us little good to still have that instrument in the hallway and can't even call one neighbor."

"I know," said Daisy. "I remember using it when I was a little girl, but people let the lines go down. It was each family's responsibility to keep the lines and poles in repair. Maybe one of these days Southern Bell will extend their lines out this far."

"I hope so," said Elizabeth.

The next day, Daisy couldn't stand it any longer. "Adam, let's you and I take the truck and go to Gulf where the train freight comes in and see if your bicycle has arrived."

When they got to the freight office, Mr. Cox, the man in charge, said, "Adam, I mailed you a card this morning to notify you that a bicycle had arrived for you. That's a nice Christmas present, but I don't know how folks can afford such frivolous things these days with the price of cotton bein' what it 'tis."

"Mr. Cox, we didn't have to buy this bicycle, I won it by writing an essay."

"Well, congratulations, son. You must be a right smart boy to do that."

"He is," replied Daisy. "He works hard at school and at home. He wants to be a farmer when he is grown up and that's what his essay was about."

"Your great granddaddy would have been proud of you. Now let's get that bicycle loaded on the truck, or do you want to ride it home?"

"Could I, Mother? I'd like to stop by and show it to some of the neighbors."

"Well, yes, you may, just don't be too late, those chores will be waiting. I have to stop by the grocery store on my way home. It sure is a beauty, red and white are my favorite colors for a bicycle. Looks like a good brand, too. Should last for years if you take good care of it. Do you know how to ride it?"

"Sure, I do. David Brown taught me on his."

"Be careful and I'll see you at home, and thanks, Mr. Cox."

"You're welcome, and congratulations, Adam."

Daisy breathed a sigh of relief as she jumped into the truck. "If that wasn't an answer to prayer I don't know what I'd call it," she mused to herself.

The next few days were exciting for everyone. Aunt Lillie Fern made the kitchen a wonderful place to walk through with all the odors of Christmas baking. Cookies, candies, pumpkin pies, mincemeat pies, popcorn balls and her very special coconut cake on which she had spent hours grating the coconut. The girls had helped her.

The Christmas program at church was very touching to each of them, reminding them of the real meaning of Christmas. Bo even went along and sat on the back row. He slipped out of the church as the last carol was sung, and waited for the Pate family at the truck. Each child received a treat bag, a tradition in the church that had been carried on for many years. A brown paper bag with an apple, an orange, nuts and hard candy made the children very happy. All the children received gifts from their Sunday School teachers. Elizabeth's teacher, Mrs. White, gave her a dainty china tea set that she could treasure all her life.

Finally, it was December 25th. Everyone was up early. A fire in the fireplace in the parlor had been kept going all night by Daisy so the room was warm and cozy. Adam had brought his new bicycle into the parlor. The stockings were hanging from the mantle and each child ran to see what was in his. There were nuts, peppermint candy sticks, an orange and a tangerine in each one. Just beneath each stocking were the gifts that Santa Claus had brought. Underneath the tree were the wrapped gifts. The Pate family tradition was for the children to see what Santa brought, then go do their chores, have breakfast and then open the wrapped gifts, making the Christmas extend a little longer.

Daisy and Lillie Fern worked diligently in the kitchen fixing their Christmas dinner. Then the aunts, uncles and cousins from the city began to arrive. Lots of hugs, kisses and more gifts were given.

After they all gathered around the big dining room table, Great Uncle Ed read the account of the birth of Christ from the Second Chapter of Luke, then prayed a long prayer. A bountiful meal was enjoyed by all. Aunt Dora had made her very special fruitcake and added it to all the other desserts.

After all the dishes had been washed, everyone gathered around the piano in the parlor and sang Christmas carols. Several of the children gave recitations they had memorized. Then they were excused to go play.

That night after everyone had gone to bed, Daisy sat down in her favorite chair in the parlor and looked at the tree. Her thoughts were of Joe and how he would have enjoyed this Christmas with the family.

CHAPTER 7

One Saturday in March, Billy Joe had the opportunity to go to Jonesboro to see an exhibition baseball game. His favorite team was playing and he asked Adam if he could borrow his bicycle. Adam said yes, if he would take good care of it. Billy Joe started out early. The sky was cloudy, but no one thought it would rain. He got to the ballpark in Jonesboro and had a chance to get the autograph of some of the players. He got a hotdog and a coke for lunch and settled down to watch the game. He noticed that the air seemed to be getting cooler and the clouds were darker. The whole sky suddenly turned a dark gray. The game continued while big blobs of white wet snowflakes began to fall.

The man sitting next to Billy Joe said, "Can you believe this, it's snowing in March."

Everyone became very excited and many people began to leave.

Billy Joe thought of his long ride home on Adam's bicycle and he thought he had better leave as much as he wanted to see the game. At least his team was winning. He went out to where he had parked the bicycle. "I'm going to be awfully mad if this stuff stops in a few minutes, but from the looks of the sky, I don't think it will," he said out loud.

As he rode out of the park a man in a pickup truck stopped and said, "Son, which way are you going?"

"I'm going toward Rocky Point," he replied.

"Put your bicycle on the truck, I'll take you as far as the crossroads at Six Forks."

"Thank you, Mister. That would help me a lot." After carefully placing Adam's bicycle on the truck, he hopped into the cab beside the stranger.

"Wish we could have stayed for the whole game," the man said. "But I'm afraid this weather is goin' to get worse before it gets better."

The road was beginning to get slick and the man was having trouble seeing. It took what seemed a long time to Billy Joe to get to Six Forks. He thanked the man and got the bicycle off the truck.

"Hope you get home all right," the man said. "I'd take you all the way, but I'd better get on to my place. My wife and younguns' are by themselves."

Billy Joe realized that the snow was too deep and the road too slick to ride the bicycle, so he began to push it. He was cold and getting wet. He realized he wan't dressed for snowy weather. He saw a house and recognized it as Rassie Crabtree's. The smoke curling from the chimney looked warn and inviting.

"I'd better stop here," Billy Joe said out loud. "He's such a grouchy old man, I wonder if he will even let me in. I've always been scared of his dogs."

He pushed the bicycle up to the door of the rundown old house that was more of a shack then a house. Old license plates were nailed all around the door. He knocked and from inside the heard a dog bark and another one growled and a gruff voice said, "Shut up and get back." An old man with a gray beard and brown stains of tobacco juice running from the corners of his mouth barely stuck his head out of the creaky old door that was about to fall off its hinges. "What you want, boy?"

Billy Joe was so scared he could hardly speak. "Mr. Crabtree, I'm Billy Joe Pate and I'm caught out in the snow and can't make it home. I was wondering if I could come in out of the storm."

"Come on in,"

"Can I bring the bicycle in too? It's my brother's and I'm trying to take good care of it."

"That'll be all right."

Billy Joe pushed the bicycle into the house. It was so dark he almost could not see where to park it.

"You is cold and wet, come on over by the far and git warm."

The two big dogs growled and began to circle around Billy Joe, looking him over.

"Will they hurt me?"

"Naw, not as long as I'm here. Go lay down, Skip and Fuzzy. We's got company."

Billy Joe got up close to the fire and took his wet jacket off and hung it over the back of a rickety old chair.

"I know my Mama is going to be worried about me, but I think she'd know I'd take shelter some place. This sure is an unexpected storm, snow coming in March."

"I've seen it snow before in March, but this one is a doozy, Rassie replied. "I'm about to eat a bite of supper. I have enough for you. Come on and pull up a chair."

The table was so cluttered it was hard for Billy Joe to find a place. Rassie put a cracked green plate in front of him along with a crooked old fork.

"Here's some hot cornbread and a jar of molasses. Pour some in yo' plate and put you some butter in it and sop it with yo' cornbread. I just made some coffee. Hope you like it."

Billy Joe was so cold and hungry that the food and coffee looked good to him in spite of the filth that surrounded it.

After stirring two heaping spoonfuls of sugar into his cup, Rassie poured his coffee into a saucer and blew on it before picking it up to drink from it. Billy Joe thought he'd better do the same thing. It was sort of hard at first, but he was getting good at it by the time he had finished the whole cup.

Rassie cleared the plates from the cluttered table and decided he would wait until morning to wash them. "I'll melt up some snow and make me some buckets of water. I haft to carry all my water from the spring down the hill and I'm glad when it snows and rains so I can save me up some water. Funny thing I never have seen a spring that twern't down at the bottom o' a hill."

"Whose boy did you say you is?"

"I'm Billy Joe Pate. My Daddy is dead. His name was Joe Pate. My Mother is Daisy Pate. We live on my Grandpa's place over by Copper Crick."

"I remember him. Whatever happened to one of his girls named Lillie Fern? I went to school with her, then I quit to help my Pa farm."

"Aunt Lillie Fern lives with us now. She worked in Washington, D. C. for a Senator until she retired."

"Did she ever marry?"

"No, she calls herself an old maid, but she doesn't act old. She's nice to have around. She likes baseball almost as much as I do. You know, she used to get to see some of the big league games when she lived in Washington. She got to see Ty Cobb play!" Billy Joe's voice became excited.

"I used ter like baseball when I was a boy, but hits been a long time since I seen a game."

"The game I went to today was getting exciting when the snow came and ruined it. I wonder who would have won."

"Let's have some music," Rassie said. He put another log on the fire and took down a very old banjo that was hanging on a nail on the unpainted wall. "I likes to pick a little ever night before I goes to bed. Don't usually have nobody to play for 'cepting these two old dogs."

He started off by picking "Old Joe Clark." He sang it in his scratchy voice,

Old Joe Clark was a fine ol' man.
He washed his face in the frying pan.
Combed his hair with a wagon wheel.
And died with the toothache in his heel.

Billy Joe started patting his foot and singing along. The dogs got up from in front of the fireplace and got under the table to get farther away from the sound.

Rassie picked and sang for almost an hour. The clock on the mantle struck 8:00.

"Well, it's almost my bedtime," Rassie announced as he carefully hung the banjo back on the wall. "If'n you need to relieve erself there's a pot in the hall behind the staircase. This ol' house is big, but I only live in these two rooms. Too much to heat and to keep. I looked after my Ma until she died. She used to keep all this old house. I git lonesome here by myself. You can sleep on the cot over there. Here's one of the quilts Ma made." He took it out of a trunk.

Billy Joe was so tired he could have slept on the floor. The fire was dying and Rassie piled ashes on the coals to keep them alive so he could add wood in the morning and revive the fire. He opened the door to see if it had stopped snowing. Billy Joe could see that it had stopped and a bright moon was shining on the beautiful white world.

The next morning he awakened when Rassie was building the fire in the cook stove and piling kindling on the coals in the fireplace and humming a tune that Billy Joe recognized as one of the hymns they sang in church on Sunday.

"Did yo' sleep good?" Rassie asked.

"I sure did."

"We'll have some breakfast here in a minute."

Rassie got out a black iron frying pan and placed it on the stove. He cut some fatback meat into thin slices and soon it was sizzling in the pan. The dogs began to wake as they smelled the aroma.

"You're hungry, too," Rassie said. "Here's some cornbread and some milk for ye'." He poured it into a pan and the two dogs greedily ate it and licked the pan clean.

"They sure do get along good together," Billy Joe said.

"I raised both of 'em from pups. They are just like two brothers. I'll let them out in the snow to run awhile. They's alwas' liked snow. I like it myself, but I'm glad when it's gone. This looks like it's here to stay awhile, even if'n it is March. I hope it ain't goin' ter hurt the fruit trees and some other stuff that a buddin' out."

"Mama always says snow is good for the wheat crop. We've got several acres planted this year. We have a colored man living on our place and he sure has helped my Mama with the plowing and planting. He aimed to plow the cornfields this week. Won't be long until time to plant corn and cotton. I'm glad we don't raise tobacco. That's an all year round job."

"Brings in good money," Rassie said, turning the meat over in the pan. "But it sure is hard work. My Paw used to raise a little patch just to keep himself in smoking tobacco. Me, I like to chaw. Never did take up smoking. Maw used ter say if God intended for man to smoke, He would'a put a chimney at the back o' his haid." He let out a long laugh as he placed the browned meat on a plate –"I'll make us some milk gravy and I'm warming up some biscuits from yesterday, and the coffee about ready."

"You sure are a good cook, Mr. Rassie," Billy Joe said, as he watched him make the gravy. "How did you learn?"

"From watching my Maw, I guess. When you don't have no wife to cook for you, you have to learn to do fer yourself."

After breakfast Rassie told Billy Joe that he had something to show him. He opened a door across the front hall. It had probably once been a parlor room, but now it was a workroom. Everywhere Billy Joe looked there were clocks – tall ones that stood on the floor and the mantle above the fireplace was lined with clocks.

"What in the world are you doing with all these clocks!" Billy Joe exclaimed.

"I work on them for people. Some of them are my own, but most are ones I haft to repair for folks. It's kind of cold to work on them this kin' of weather, but soon as it warms up, I'll git in here and git to workin'. I sometimes start me a fire in that old wood stove, but hit takes a lot of wood, and I ain't as able as I used ter be to cut and haul wood."

Billy Joe said," We have a grandfather's clock that hasn't run in years. Reckon you could work on it?"

"I could try."

"I'll tell Mama, and maybe she can bring it over here in the truck. That reminds me, I guess I'd better try to make it on home. She might be getting worried about me. Can I leave the bicycle here?"

"Sure. I'll take good care of it. Here, you better wear one of my boggin' caps and mittens, and some old galoshes, and here's a sweater to put on over your jacket. It's cold out thar."

"Thank you, Mr. Rassie. I'll bring these things back when I come to get the bicycle. I appreciate all you have done for me."

"My pleasure, son, it was good to have some company."

He pulled the galoshes over his shoes. They were big, but would help to keep his feet dry and from getting so cold. The snow was deep and Billy Joe found walking was slow going. After walking about fifteen minutes, he heard a loud noise behind. It was the county snowplow. The big yellow machine that usually scraped the dirt roads was scraping the snow to one side of the road.

"Billy Joe Pate, is that you," Mr. Hales shouted down from his high seat on the tractor.

"Yes, sir, Mr. Hales. Could I get a ride? This snow sure is deep and cold."

"Climb on up. I'm not supposed to let anybody ride on this contraption with me, but I'm going to do it this time anyhow." He spat a long stream of brown tobacco juice that landed on the white snow and wiped his mouth with his gloved hand. "What you doin' out in this here snow so early in the mornin'? I know you're not on your way to Sunday school as I know for a fact that ain't no church havin' meetin' this mornin'."

"I went to a baseball game in Jonesboro and got caught in the snow. I spent the night at Rassie Crabtree's house."

"You mean you spent the night with that crazy ol' man and his dogs?"

"Sure did and he's not crazy. I had a good time. He can pick the banjo and he works on clocks."

"Guess I've just heard folks talk about him. My Paw knew his Paw and he always said the whole Crabtree family were all on the strange side—ol' man Crabtree was part Indian, that's where he got his name Crabtree—some folks say they should have been called Crabapple, they were so crabby." He let out another stream of tobacco juice and a laugh to go with it.

The snowplow sent snow flying up almost as high as the seats that Billy Joe and Mr. Hales were perched on. "Is this thing hard to drive?" Billy Joe asked.

"Not too bad, but it's harder in this snow than it is when I'm scraping dirt roads."

"Do you like this job?"

"Yes, I like it. Pays pretty good and helps me feed my wife and six younguns. My girl, Emma Lou, is in your class at school, ain't she?"

"Yes, sir."

"She says you are a good baseball player."

"Yes, sir, I like to play baseball. I hope some day to be a big league player. I'd rather do that than farm. My brother Adam likes to farm."

"I don't like it either. That's why I like this job. I get to go all over the county and I get to ride." He laughed again. "It's better than followin' behind a mule."

They arrived at the driveway to the Pate house. "I'll just plow out y'all's driveway. Your Maw might need to get the truck out."

The noise from the snowplow brought all the Pates out onto the front porch.

Billy Joe jumped down from his seat and ran up the steps that had already been shoveled and right into the arms of his Mother.

"Where have you been, Billy Joe? We've been so worried about you."

"Thank you, Albert, for bringing my boy home," Daisy shouted above the noisy engine.

"You're welcome, Daisy."

"Could I offer you a cup of hot chocolate or coffee?"

"I reckon not," Albert replied. "I've got an awful lot of roads to scrape today."

They all went into the house. Billy Joe took off all the clothes that belonged to Rassie.

"Where did you get these clothes and where is my bicycle?" Adam asked.

"I spent the night with Mr. Rassie Crabtree and your bicycle is at his house. He loaned me these clothes."

"You mean you spent the night at Rassie Crabtree's," Adam said as his eyes grew wide and his mouth dropped open.

"And he did not eat you alive?" Elizabeth chimed in. "My friend Betty Lou Hill at school says he grabs children and they are never seen anymore."

"Aw, that's not true, Elizabeth," Billy Joe said. "He's a nice man, and wouldn't hurt anybody. His dogs even got to where they liked me."

"I don't care where you spent the night. I'm just glad you are safe and sound," Daisy said. "This snow was unexpected or I would have never let you go to Jonesboro."

"Mama, Mr. Rassie fixes clocks and I told him about our grandfather clock, and he said you should bring it to him and let him see if he can fix it. Maybe we could take it when we go get Adam's bicycle."

"Yes, I knew he fixed clocks. I just never have taken anything to him."

"Mama, it's so strange—the part of the house that he and the dogs live in isn't very well kept, but the room that the clocks are in is clean and well organized. It looked like a different world. Mr. Hales said the Crabtrees were all crazy and that Mr. Rassie's father was an Indian."

"I can tell you about the Crabtrees," Aunt Lillie Fern spoke up. I was in school with Rassie when we were in the lower grades. Yes, his father was part Indian, Cherokee, I understand. His mother was one of the Siler girls. He came to this county not long after the Civil War. He went to work for Mr. Tom Siler who had six daughters. Each one of the girls began to get married and leave home and there was only one left—Mary. She wasn't very pretty and she had what folks called a clubbed foot. She was born with one leg shorter than the other and she always walked with a limp. Mr. Siler was sure that no man would ever want her as a wife. So when Solomon Crabtree came riding up on a beautiful horse and asked Mr. Siler for work on his farm, he thought maybe this is the man that would like to marry his Mary. He introduced them, knowing that most people in these parts didn't think too highly of white folks marrying Indians. But he told Solomon that he could marry her if he would work for him for seven years. Well, ol' Sol fell madly in love with Mary and agreed to work the seven years. However, after about five years Mr. Siler died and Solomon and Mary got in the buggy and went off to another state and got married. They came back to Mr. Siler's land and farmed it until they died. They had the one child, Rassie. He is about my age. We were in school and one day some people got the notion that Indian children should not go to school with white children. This really made Solomon Crabtree mad and he stomped up to the school, got Rassie by the hand and told the principal in no uncertain terms that he did not want his son to go to a school where he was not wanted and he could always use him to work on the farm. Rassie left and never came back again. He went away to Chicago or some place for a few years and he came home when his father died and lived with his mother and took care of her until she died. I think while he was away was when he learned to work on clocks. He has let the farm grow up in weeds, sold off the horses and other farm animals. He never married and like his father has had little to do with other folks.

"Well, he certainly was good to me, and fed me real well. He's a good cook," Billy Joe said as he ate a big piece of Aunt Lillie Fern's devil's food cake and drank hot chocolate. "Can we make some snow cream after while?"

"We sure will," Daisy said, giving him a big hug.

CHAPTER 8

One day after all the snow was gone and the spring plowing was done, Daisy was sitting in a rocker on the front porch resting a few minutes after lunch.

A car came up the driveway. It was a yellow two-door Ford with a rumble seat and it had the canvas top down, a convertible. A nice looking, well-dressed man in a white shirt and navy blue pants and a bright necktie got out. He slipped into a navy blue and green checked sports coat, picked up a black briefcase and walked up to the porch steps.

"Afternoon, ma'am," tipping his light colored straw hat that had a navy blue band around it, "My name is Jeremiah Bradshaw. Most people call me Jerry. And whom am I speaking to?" he asked.

"Daisy Pate, glad to meet you. What are you selling?"

"How do you know that I'm selling something?" he laughed. When he did his blue eyes behind rimless glasses twinkled and a dimple in each cheek showed.

"Your briefcase gave you away," Daisy replied.

"Oh! This"–he opened the briefcase that was filled with several catalogs. "I'm from the Powers Lightning Rod Company. Mind if I sit down and show you some of our wares?"

"You may," Daisy said, pointing to another rocking chair. Suddenly she felt her face flush and she reached up to pat her hair that was coming loose from the ball on the back of her head.

"I noticed when I drove up that you do not have lightning rods on your house.'

"No, we don't. This house used to belong to my Grandfather and he never believed in having those things on his roof."

"Some folks feel that way, but I know for a fact that they can ward off lightning. With summer coming on you know we will have thunder and lightning storms. It's a good time of year to get prepared."

"You might as well shut your briefcase and be on your way," Daisy said in a shy voice. "I don't have any money and won't until next Fall when I sell my crops."

"Why, Mrs. Pate, don't even think about money right now. Where is Mr. Pate? Is he out in one of the fields?"

"My husband passed away some time ago."

"I'm so sorry to hear that." He got up from his chair and patted her on the shoulder. "You run this farm all alone?"

"I have some help and my four children help, too."

"You are a brave lady. How many acres do you have here?"

"Oh, about 300. I inherited it from my Grandfather."

"That's a lot of land to take care of. Have you ever thought of selling off some of it?"

"That has never entered my mind. It has been in my peoples' possession for generations. In fact, this land was a land grant from King George of England. Not many people have been able to hang onto theirs, especially after the Civil War. My great grandfather fought in the war and my great grandmother kept this farm going in spite of Sherman's march through the South. My Grandfather told me all sorts of stories that they told him when he was a boy."

"You ought to write a book about those stories."

"Maybe I will someday when I have time." Daisy felt her heart sort of flutter as she hung onto every word that Jerry was saying. He rattled on about the safety of having lightning rods on your house and on your barn." "Mind if I take a look at your barn?" he said.

They strolled down to the barn and Jerry walked around the big barn measuring it with his eye. "I think you could do with about six rods, maybe eight," he said.

"I told you that I don't have any money."

"That's okay. I can take your order now and have the rods installed and you won't have to make a payment until September or October. Our company will allow you to make payments without paying any interest."

"About how much money are we talking about?" Daisy asked.

Jerry took out a pen and figured on a piece of paper. "Now, let's see, the rods are $32.00, the ground wires are $5.00 and labor for installation is 75 cents per hour. It will probably take about four hours. That is $3.00 more. With transportation by train of the rods from our plant in Ohio, it comes to $45.00. Think you could swing that?"

Daisy was so enamored with his voice she nodded her head yes before she allowed what he was saying to sink into her brain.

As they walked back to the house, Daisy found herself asking him if he would like to have a glass of lemonade and a piece of Aunt Lillie Fern's pound cake.

"Sounds good to me," Jerry replied. They went into the kitchen. "Where is your Aunt?"

"She is taking her afternoon nap. Where are you staying, Mr. Bradshaw?"

"I'm at Mrs. Enloe's boarding house in town."

"Do you get your meals there?"

"I'm gone about all day and do try to get back there for supper. Mrs. Enloe is such a good cook so I really do not like to miss one of her suppers. You Southern ladies sure do know how to cook. This cake is delicious. Mind if I have another piece?"

"Help yourself. How long are you going to stay in this part of North Carolina?"

"Probably several more weeks."

"You must come have supper with us one night or even better come have Sunday dinner with us. You could attend church with us. I'd like for you to meet my Aunt and my children."

"I'd like that very much. I get lonely on Sundays. I make out fine during the week as I am so busy selling lightning rods."

"Well, you just come on over this Sunday morning. Sunday school starts at 10:00 and preaching at 11:00. We go to the Quaker Meeting just down the road."

"I passed by that church on my way here. Beautiful place. Would you believe it, I'm a member of a Quaker Meeting back in Ohio."

He drove away in his yellow Ford after he had filled out the paper work for the lightning rod order.

Daisy waived to him. "What a nice man" she thought. She couldn't quite understand the feelings she was having. "I'm looking forward to Sunday," she said out loud to herself.

"And why is that?" asked Aunt Lillie Fern as she came out the door with her sewing basket in her hand.

"We're going to have company on Sunday, a nice man, Jeremiah Bradshaw, who just left. He is here from Ohio and he sells lightning rods. Said he was a Quaker and I asked him to go to Meeting with us and come home with us for dinner. And he accepted my invitation," Daisy replied, smiling.

"Why Daisy Pate, that smile on your face is very becoming. We'll have to kill one or two of those pullets and fry up some chicken for this man. Did you ask him if he was married and had a family?"

"No, I didn't even think of that."

Sunday came and Jeremiah met them at the meeting house. He appeared even more immaculately dressed than when Daisy had seen him before. He had on a tan suit with a matching vest. His white shirt collar looked starched stiff and his necktie appeared to be pure silk with a pattern that made his suit even more outstanding. He had on brown and white wing-tipped shoes.

After introducing him to her family, Daisy proudly walked into the sanctuary beside him. Heads turned to see the stranger. Several ladies whispered to one another behind their cardboard funeral home fans that had a picture of Jesus holding a lamb in His arm. After the opening exercise, which consisted of a hymn, a prayer, a few announcements, the congregation went into their age group Sunday school classes. Jeremiah followed Daisy into a room that had a circle of chairs. Mr. Thomas, the teacher, came in, introduced himself to Jeremiah, shaking his hand and telling him how glad he was to have him. Several people recognized him as the "lightning rod salesman" who had been by their homes. When the class was over they all went back into the sanctuary.

Daisy said, "I forgot to tell you that we don't have a full-time minister. We only have preaching every other Sunday. Today we have what we call "Sit Still Meetin'. I suppose in Ohio you call it "Open Worship.""

"Yes, that's what we call it," Jeremiah replied.

The children and Aunt Lillie Fern joined them and all sat on the same bench. It was sort of a tight squeeze and it caused Daisy to sit very close to Jeremiah. It felt good to her to be near such a well-dressed fellow who smelled like Burma shave lotion. It reminded her of when she was younger and had a date with a city boy that was visiting his aunt in the community. He had kissed her when they were playing the game "Spin the Bottle" at a party. She had pretended she didn't like it.

They all sat quietly waiting for someone to speak. Not a sound was heard until Mr. Ralph Hicks stood to his feet and read a verse from The Psalms and with a solemn face and a quivering voice expanded for five minutes on what the verse meant to him and his life. He sat down and Mr. Gilmore Hudson called out a song from the hymnal. Because this was a Quaker meeting, the piano was not used and the congregation sang it a cappella. Jeremiah joined in, singing the tenor part while Daisy's alto blended well with him. They smiled at each other when the hymn ended.

Quietness again fell over the crowd. Sister Bessie Simmons, sitting in her usual place on the second row on the right hand side, began to quiver as she became so filled with the Spirit and gave real meaning as to why this particular denomination who started out to be called The Society of Friends, got the name of Quakers. Her whole body was quaking as the Spirit moved her. Her husband, Rudolph Simmons, sat next to her with his head bowed and his eyes closed. It was hard for the Pate children to keep their heads bowed in reverence while Sister Simmons quaked.

Finally one of the men seated in a chair up on the pulpit stand arose and said, "Let us be dismissed with a word of prayer. All stand, please." They stood up and he prayed for what seemed like ten minutes, ending with, "Now we will be dismissed by shaking hands with seven people in our Quaker tradition, Amen."

Daisy and the family had walked to church. Since Jeremiah had his Ford convertible there, he offered them a ride. The children squeezed into the rumble seat with the youngest sitting on the oldest ones lap. Daisy and Aunt Lillie Fern sat up front with Jeremiah.

Daisy and Lillie Fern and the girls scurried around to get lunch on the table while the boys entertained Jeremiah on the porch. They were full of questions as it wasn't often that they had a man to talk with who would have been about their Father's age. They each let him know how much they missed their Dad.

Billy Joe asked him if he had ever seen a major league baseball game. He said he had and that he liked the game. Of course, that pleased Billy Joe.

During the afternoon, they all gathered around the piano. Aunt Lillie Fern played and they all sang together. It was amazing how well Daisy and Jeremiah's voices blended.

Too soon for Daisy, it was time to go to the barn to milk the cows, feed the hogs, chickens and mules and gather the eggs. Jeremiah excused himself and departed after going on and on about the wonderful meal and the good time he had. "I'll drop by and see all of you sometime this week when I am working out this way," he promised.

As Daisy was tucking the girls into bed that night, Lizzy asked, "Mama, are you going to marry Mr. Bradshaw?"

"Why, what would make you think such a thing, Lizzy?"

"I don't know, Mommy. He is a nice man and I wish I had a daddy like other girls." A lump came up in Daisy's throat and she swallowed hard before telling Lizzy to say her prayers.

On Wednesday afternoon about 5:00 o'clock Jeremiah came driving up. Lillie Fern was the only one in the house. He knocked on the door and she answered, "Hello, come in."

"I was in this neighborhood and thought I'd stop by and see if you were going to prayer meeting tonight."

"Everyone is out at the barn doing his chores. I'm getting supper on the table; would you like to stay and eat with us? I've cooked a big pot of pinto beans and a pan of cornbread."

"I don't want to be any trouble."

"No trouble, I'll just set another plate."

"Mighty generous of you, ma'am."

About that time, Lizzy came in with a basket of eggs. Daisy carrying a bucket of milk blushed when she saw Jeremiah standing in the kitchen. Her first thought was he must think I look a mess with these dirty work clothes and this old hat on my head. I must look like a real hillbilly to him in his immaculate clothing.

Lillie Fern took the pail of milk and began to strain it through a clean white piece of cheesecloth into a gray crock.

"So that's how you do the milk." At home we get it delivered to our front porch every morning from the milk truck," Jeremiah chuckled.

Daisy excused herself and ran into her bedroom to change her clothes and comb her hair.

"Jeremiah is going to eat supper with us and wants to go to prayer meeting," Lillie Fern told Daisy when she returned to the kitchen.

"That's great," Daisy said, trying not to sound overly enthusiastic.

"I don't think I'll go to prayer meeting," Lillie Fern said. "I'm rather tired tonight and I feel like I might be taking a cold."

"Mother, I have a book report to finish," Mary Lou said. "Could I stay home with Aunt Lillie?"

"May I stay home, too," Lizzy begged.

"Since you can ride with Mr. Bradshaw and won't be walking," Adams said, "Could Billy Joe and I stay home as we both have tests tomorrow that we need to study for."

"Oh! All right, but let's don't make a habit of missing our Wednesday night prayer meeting."

Daisy got into the car with Jeremiah. They talked very little on the short ride to the church.

After the hour-long prayer meeting, Jerry looked at his watch and said to Daisy, "How about let's you and I go over to Hopkinsville and get a cone of ice cream?"

"Oh! That's about six miles from here; it would throw me so late getting home to see if the children have finished their lessons and are in bed."

"Don't worry, I'm sure your Aunt has seen to it that they turn in early. We won't be gone all that long. Come on, let's do something fun for a change."

They got into the Ford and Jerry drove quickly to what was known to the folks in Hopkinsville as the Circle In because it sat in the middle of an intersection of two highways. The young folks would say, "Let's go to the Circle In and then we can circle out." It was a hangout for young people.

Jerry said he would go in and get the ice cream. He asked what kind Daisy would like and she chose strawberry. He came out with cones piled high. He, too, had chosen strawberry. They sat in the car and licked their ice cream, commenting on how good it was.

They drove back to Daisy's house, talking and laughing like two teenagers on a date. Before they got out of the car, Jerry leaned over and said, "Daisy, may I kiss you goodnight?"

Before she realized it, Daisy leaned forward and allowed him to kiss her on the lips. It felt good to her and it felt right.

The next morning at breakfast the children teased Daisy about having a date when she told them they had been to the Circle In for ice cream.

"That is where I am going on my first date," Mary Lou announced.

"I think you have a few years to wait for that," Daisy replied.

For the next couple of weeks Jerry stopped by regularly. During this time Daisy became even more fond of him. Then suddenly without even a goodbye he didn't come anymore. Daisy and the family wondered what had happened to him, but assumed he had moved on to some other place to sell lightning rods.

One day a letter came addressed to Mrs. Daisy Pate. It was postmarked Dayton, Ohio. It didn't have a return address. "This must be from Jerry as we don't know anyone else from Ohio."

With trembling fingers she opened the letter. Tears filled her eyes as she read the words.

Mrs. Pate,

This is to inform you that I am Jeremiah Bradshaw's legal wife. I found your name and address inside one of his coat pockets upon his return from North Carolina.

When I confronted him, he said you and your family had been kind to him, invited him to church and Sunday dinner. I thank you very much for your kindness to him. However, this isn't the first letter that I have had to write to his so-called friends. Being a traveling salesman, he is away from home a great deal of the time. Everywhere he goes, he attaches himself to a family and then leaves without a word. I don't suppose he told you about me or our three children. I do not know what sort of relationship you had with him, but I know how charming he can be. You probably wonder why I put up with his shenanigans; well, I love him very much and he makes a good living for me and our children.

Please do not ever try to contact him. Some women have, and I put a stop to it right away.

It was signed, *The Wife of a Lightning Rod Salesman*

Daisy sat down in the rocking chair on the porch, the same one she sat in the day that this charming man came into their lives.

"Well, I never," she said out loud.

"You never what?" Aunt Lillie asked.

"That lightning rod salesman is a married man with three children. He came around here acting like a single man, trying to court me, a widow!" She handed Lillie the letter.

After reading it, Lillie said, "I thought he was too good to be true. I'm glad you found out about him before you became too deeply involved."

"Let's don't tell the children about this. I don't want them to know how gullible their mother is," Daisy said, as she tore the letter into bits. "From now on I'll be very cautious about door-to-door salesmen. Oh! here comes that flittery old Watkins Liniment man. You talk to him, Aunt Lillie, and tell him we don't need anything today. I'm going in the house; I've had it with salesmen."

CHAPTER 9

One day in spring before school was out, Lizzy and Mary Lou had to walk home from school alone. Billy Joe had a baseball game at another school and Adam had gone along with the team to cheer him on.

When they came to a fork in the road, their friend, Jenny, and her older sister Madge, left them to walk the remainder of the way home by themselves. They did not know that convicts from the county jail were working on the road. They saw a man with a shotgun guarding the men. They had been warned by their Mother to never get close to those men who had on striped uniforms working on the roads. The men were on both sides of the road cleaning out ditches with rakes and shovels.

The girls had to walk between the rows of men. They were scared and stayed close together and walked as fast as they could to get by them. Just as they got to the end of the row, the last man reached out and grabbed Mary Lou with his right arm. Holding her in front of him, he quickly ran into the woods. The guard lifted his shotgun to shoot but was afraid he would hit the girl. Mary Lou was screaming, Lizzy was screaming, "Let my sister go." The guard held the gun on the other prisoners to keep them from running away. "I'll shoot the first man that moves."

Lizzy ran as fast as she could, screaming all the way. She was only about a quarter of a mile from home. Daisy heard her screams, jumped up from the flowerbed that she had been weeding.

Running to Lizzy she gathered her in her arms and asked what was the matter and where was Mary Lou?

Lizzy breathlessly told her mother what had happened. Daisy reeled from the impact of her words.

"Bo," she screamed, "Come here quick."

Realizing the terror in her voice, the black man dropped the shovel he was using and ran quickly toward her.

"A convict grabbed Mary Lou and ran off into the woods with her. What are we going to do?"

"Maybe he won't hurt her, he just wants her for a hostage. I'll go into them woods and see if'n I can find them. You get the truck and go to the nearest neighbor and have them go fetch the sheriff. Then come back here and get yo' rifle and don't be afraid to shoot 'em if you see 'em." Bo grabbed a new ax handle that Daisy had bought to put into her favorite ax. It was a solid piece of wood and could be used as a club if necessary.

Daisy told Lizzy to go in the house and tell Aunt Lillie Fern to get the rifle from up above the kitchen door and load it and to lock all the doors in the house.

Fortunately, Daisy had the truck keys in her pocket. The truck was usually hard to start but this time it started at the first turn of the ignition.

"This is when we need telephones in this community," Daisy said out loud.

She drove quickly to the nearest neighbors' house, blew the horn and out onto the front porch came Mr. And Mrs. Jones. She quickly explained what had happened and asked Mr. Jones to drive the three miles to Mr. Berry's store to use his phone to call the sheriff and to tell anyone he saw to come help look for the man and Mary Lou.

She turned the truck around and headed back home. "What can I do to help my child?" she wailed. "All I can do is pray. I'll pray that he doesn't hurt my baby and that she will be found alive." All sorts of horrible thoughts began to run through Daisy's mind.

She returned home to find a frightened Lizzy and Aunt Lillie Fern.

"I've got to do something," Daisy said frantically. "I'm going to take the rifle and go into the woods. Perhaps Bo has found them and will need my help. I have never shot anyone in my life, but maybe I can make him turn Mary Lou loose if he sees the gun."

Grabbing some extra bullets, she took off in the direction that Bo had gone. She made her way through the thick woods, looking cautiously in every direction. Suddenly she saw Bo. "Have you seen anybody?"

"No, ma'am, I ain't."

"We've got to keep looking."

Before they could go much farther they saw Sheriff Ferrell and at least six men coming toward them.

"Daisy, have you seen anything yet?" he asked.

"No," sobbed Daisy." I'm so glad to see you and all these men."

"We'll spread out and comb these woods good. Daisy, you and Bo go on back home in case he shows up there with Mary Lou. Besides, I know it's getting time to do up your farm chores."

"Please find them, Thomas," she pleaded. "It's time to go milk and feed the stock. How can I think of anything like that when my baby is missing?"

"Come on, Miz Pate, you's go home and git that work done up."

As they came out of the woods, Adam and Billy Joe came running to them.

"What's the sheriff's car and all these other cars doing up on the main road?" Billy Joe asked. "Mama, why are you carrying the rifle?"

She handed the rifle to Bo and ran to the boys, gathering them in her arms. Through her tears, she told what had happened.

"Give me that rifle, Bo. I'll go after him," Adam shouted.

"No, Adam," Daisy said. "The sheriff and his men are hunting through the woods where he carried Mary Lou."

"Is Lizzy okay?" Billy Joe asked.

"Just scared like the rest of us. Bo, you take the rifle with you. Don't shoot him but make him give you Mary Lou if you should see him."

"I'll go help you," Adam said.

"I'll be there soon as I get changed from my baseball uniform," said Billy Joe.

Bo and Adam headed for the barn to feed and water the animals. Adam climbed up the ladder to the hayloft to throw down a bale of hay. He thought he heard a noise. "One of the chickens must have come up here, made a nest. She is probably one of our settin' hens. I'll look for it another time."

He started back down the ladder and suddenly he saw Mary Lou's face and a man's face peering over a bale of hay.

"Mary Lou," Adam screamed.

The man said, "Sssh, don't talk, just listen. I need some clothes. I haven't hurt your sister and if you get me some clothes so I can get out of these convicts stripes, I'll let her go and I'll be on my way."

"We don't have any men's clothes," Adam replied. "Why don't you let my sister go and turn yourself into the sheriff?"

"I can't do that. I'm sick and tired of being caged like an animal."

"He has a little girl about my age that he wants to go home to see," Mary Lou piped up.

"Our Dad is dead and we don't have any men's clothes. What did you do to get yourself in jail in the first place?" Adam asked.

"It's a long story. Maybe you could get me some women's clothes and I could slip out of here after dark."

"Women's clothes, you don't mean it. Please turn Mary Lou loose and let her go to Mama. Mama is so worried about her."

"I want my Mama," Mary Lou began to cry.

"Who you's talkin' to, Adam?" Bo asked.

Adam didn't reply.

Bo came around the side of the barn. "I thought I heered you talkin'. Was yo talking to me?"

"No," replied Adam. He climbed all the way back up the ladder. "I think we need another bale of hay. Get out of the way, Bo, I'm going to throw it down."

Bo moved back as the hay bounced to the ground. "Why you's staying in that hay loft so long? We need ter git this work done. Before hit gits dark. Them two cows need milkin'. Here comes Billy Joe wid da mulk buckets. Adam, is yo gonna milk one of dem cows and Billy Joe the tuther? I's gonna go slop dem hogs."

Billy Joe arrived at the barn. He looked up to see Adam in the loft. Adam motioned for him to come up the ladder. Adam whispered to him that the convict and Mary Lou were hiding behind some bales of hay. "What am I going to do, Billy Joe? The convict wants some clothes so he can get rid of those prison stripes, said he would even wear some women's clothes."

"I want to see Mary Lou," Billy Joe announced.

Mary Lou raised her head up. "Hey! Billy Joe, I'm okay. I just want to see Mommy."

"Okay. I'll let her go if you won't tell anybody where I'm hiding. As soon as it gets dark I'll leave."

Mary Lou, Billy Joe and Adam all scrambled down the ladder.

"Billy Joe, let's you and I milk the cows. Mary Lou, you go onto the house, but don't tell where the man is hiding," Adam said.

"But what if Mommy asks me? I can't tell a lie," Mary Lou said.

"Just say he turned you loose. You don't have to say where."

Mary Lou ran as fast as she could to the house and knocked on the back door that was locked.

"Let me in, Mommy, let me in!"

Daisy opened the door, grabbed Mary Lou, hugging her tightly and crying big tears. "I was afraid I'd never see you again. Are you hurt? Did that man hurt you?"

"No, Mommy, he didn't hurt me. Really he is a nice man."

"How can you say that when he grabbed you and carried you off into the woods?"

"His name is Bill and he didn't like being in jail. He has a little girl my age. Her name is Margaret and he wants to see her so badly, he decided he would run away and try to find her. He said her mother has taken her away and he is afraid he will never see her again. I asked him why he was in jail. He said he lost his job and didn't have any money and Margaret was hungry, so he stole some food from a grocery store and the owner of the store had him put in jail. Mommy, I told him that Jesus loves him."

"Mary Lou, you are such a good little girl with such a tender heart. I'm so proud of you," Daisy wailed through her tears. "We've got to let Thomas Ferrell know that you are safe."

"I'm so hungry, Aunt Lillie Fern. Can I have something to eat?"

"You sure can, child. I'm so glad to see you."

Lizzy came squealing into the room. "Mary Lou, Mary Lou, I'm so sorry that I couldn't help you when that mean old man grabbed you. Am I ever glad to see you."

Daisy ran outside and shouted as loud as she could, "Mary Lou is home."

One of the men came out of the woods. "What did you say?" he shouted.

"Mary Lou is home. You can call off the search."

"We still have to look for the man. It's getting dark and since she is home safely we probably won't look much more tonight. I don't think he is a dangerous person."

The boys came in with the milk and never mentioned their encounter with the man. No one asked if they had seen him.

All the family was so glad to see Mary Lou home safely. When they bowed their heads for the blessing at the supper table, each one expressed thanksgiving to God for bringing her home safely.

The next time the county newspaper came out there was a picture of Mary Lou and an article about her ordeal. It reported that the man whose names was Bill Henderson had never been found.

Secretly in her heart, Mary Lou was glad they hadn't found him and she prayed that he would someday find his little Margaret.

CHAPTER 10

"Mama, Mama," Billy Joe shouted as he ran toward the barn where Daisy was helping Bo and Adam place bales of sweet-smelling summer hay into the barn loft.

"What is it, Billy Joe?"

"The man from the Rural Electrification Association is at our house and wants to see you. He is looking around. I can't wait until we get electricity and I can listen to baseball games on the radio. I'll even be able to hear the World Series."

"I'll be there in a minute. I'm almost as excited as Billy Joe."

They hurried to the house.

"Mrs. Pate, I'm Amos Brown, an engineer for the power company and hope you will want to sign on when we bring power lines down the main road. I was just looking at the best way to bring it to your house."

"By all means, Mr. Brown, we want it. I haven't the slightest idea how much it will cost."

"Mrs. Pate, our company is a co-op. That means that each month when you pay your light bill a certain percent of it goes into the power company to help build up a reserve to help us extend electricity to more people. We would like for you to put up $50.00 in order to get the poles and lines brought from the main road to your house. However, if you don't have the cash at the moment, we can allow you to pay $4.50 each month for a year. It will be added to your regular monthly bill."

"I'd rather do it that way," Daisy replied.

"I'll draw up the papers as soon as I figure up how many poles will be needed and if a transformer will have to be placed near your house. Then you will have to sign, giving us permission to come onto your land. You know there are some people in the area that will not give us permission to come onto their land."

"How soon will we get power?" Billy Joe asked excitedly.

"We have the poles and lines and what we call a substation already in place on the main road. As soon as we get everyone that wants power in this area signed up we can work on bringing the lines to each home. Then you will have to get an electrician to come wire your house. We don't do that."

"More money," Daisy thought. "Somehow I'll get the money for it. Electricity is going to make our lives so much easier. The sooner the better," she spoke out loud.

"I'll get back with you in a few days. I can give you some names of some licensed electricians that can wire your house. You might want to get more than one estimate. Remember, there are shysters out there that will take advantage of you."

"There is a man in our church who is an electrician. His name is Paul Loudermilk. I'll speak to him about wiring our house."

"I know him, he is a good man. I'll be going along now. Good day, Mrs. Pate, Billy Joe." Mr. Brown got into his truck and left.

"He never did give us a time as to when we can turn on our lights," Billy Joe said with disappointment in his voice, "I've got to go tell Aunt Lillie Fern that we have to get her radio out of the packing box. She really has missed using it since she moved here from Washington, D. C. She will get to hear her stories in the afternoon—'Ma Perkins' and 'The Guiding Light.' She has told us all about them. I can't wait to listen to 'Lights Out' and 'The Shadow,' 'The Lone Ranger' and 'Terry and the Pirates.'"

"You sound as if you will be spending all your time listening to that radio. I think not, young man. There is still work to be done on this farm and homework for school to do."

"And baseball to play," Billy Joe said.

Daisy went back to the barn to tell Adam and Bo what was happening.

Bo said, "Mrs. Pate, do you reckon I could git the power man to run lights over ter my cabin? I shore would like it."

"Bo, I'm sorry I didn't even think of that when I was speaking to Mr. Brown. I think it could be arranged. I might have to sign for it since the cabin is on my property."

"I'll pay de bill and whatever hit costs to war tha' cabin. We had 'lectricity back where I come from and I shore miss hit."

"Can we get an electric stove?" Adam asked. "I'm so tired of chopping stove wood and carrying it in. No more kerosene lamps to fill."

"No more glass lamp globes to clean or wicks to replace or trim," Daisy echoed. "No more trips to the ice plant for ice or trips to the spring box where we keep our milk and butter. We can get Aunt Lillie Fern's refrigerator and electric lamps out of storage in the shed. You know, I believe there is an electric stove out there, too. She had all that kind of stuff in her apartment in Washington. There may be a washing machine in that big storage box. Let's finish putting this hay in the barn. I'm as excited as a kid."

"Maybe one of these days we'll get the telephone lines out here in the country," Adam said.

"Adam, I bet 'em purdy gals at school would be callin' yo all de time," Bo teased.

Daisy and Adam went to the house and found Lizzie and Mary Lou dancing all around with Aunt Lillie Fern and Billy Joe laughing and clapping.

"I didn't think I would live long enough to see this day," said Aunt Lillie Fern. "Maybe we can get a pump for the well and even put in a bathroom and a hot water heater. First thing you know we'll all be lazy when we get all these conveniences. But won't that be nice," Lilly Fern beamed.

"This is going to be a wonderful summer," Daisy mused. "I haven't seen this family so happy since—"

"Since Christmas," Mary Lou chimed.

That night after everyone was asleep, Daisy knelt by her bed to pray. She asked God to show her how she could get the money to do all that needed to be done to get the electricity brought to their farm. Immediately the thought came to her mind – she whispered out loud, "I'll sell the timber off the north side of our property. Mr.

Jones who owns a sawmill asked me about it some time ago. He said the hardwoods needed to be thinned out. I had been saving those trees for a time when I really needed the money. And right now is the time. I'll write him a letter and tell him that I am ready to sell. Thank you, Lord."

She got into bed, fell asleep and dreamed of all the wonderful things that electricity would bring to her family.

CHAPTER 11

The mailman, Charlie Jones, drove his dusty black A-model Ford into the Pate driveway and honked his horn. Aunt Lillie Fern was the only one in the house and she came out with flour on her hands.

"What's all the noise about?"

Charlie said, "Lillie Fern, you have an important-looking letter here from Washington, D.C. and I thought I'd better deliver it to you personally."

"Well, thank you, Charlie."

"Also you all got the Progressive Farmer Magazine today and a postcard from your cousin Sally over in Pleasantville. Lillie Fern, ain't you going to open your letter from Washington?"

"Not right yet, Charlie. I have flour on my hands." She turned and went back into the house, mumbling, "I don't want him to know what is in my letter. He would probably tell it all over the county."

She washed her hands and carefully opened the envelope wondering out loud, "Why is Senator Calhoun writing to me? I sent a sympathy card when his wife died." She read the letter out loud.

My dear Lillie Fern,

I know it has been a long time since I have contacted you.

As you know, my beloved Etheline passed away six months ago. I have been so lonely and heartbroken. I thought perhaps if I got in touch with you, you could console me. After all, you were my secretary for more years than I can remember. You always helped me so much when any problem arose at work or with my family. I would like very much to see you and sit down and talk. I was wondering if you could come on the train to Washington to visit me in my home. Please write back and let me know if you can come. I will be most happy to buy your train ticket.

Sincerely,
B. Calhoun

"Well, I never," Lillie Fern said thoughtfully.

"You never what?" Daisy asked, coming in the kitchen with a bucket of freshly picked green beans.

"This letter," handing it to Daisy.

Daisy read it. Turning to Lillie Fern, "Well, are you going?"

"I don't know. There is so much we need to do with all the canning and jelly making."

"Now, don't worry about that, Aunt Lillie. It sounds like the Senator needs you."

"Daisy, I've never told you or anybody about my relationship with Mr. B, as I used to call him. When I first went to Washington as a young lady fresh out of business college I was so fascinated by the political scene. Before I went to work for Mr. B. I was in the typing pool and I lived in a rooming house with several other girls in the pool. We were invited to parties and dances. Of course, with my Quaker background I would never dance, but I enjoyed talking to the Senators and their wives. That is how I met Mr. B. He was a young Senator from North Carolina and when he found out that I was from North Carolina he asked me to become his private secretary. I was so thrilled. He was so handsome and well liked by everyone. I guess I was sort of in love with him." She closed her eyes and smiled. "When I had been there about six months, Mr. B. came in one morning with a big smile on his face. I asked him why he was so happy. He told me that Miss Etheline Price, the daughter of a very wealthy Massachusetts family had promised to marry him. Of course I had to congratulate him and tell him how happy I was for him. Etheline was a very nice person and always treated me well. They had about 50 years together before she got sick and died. She was the perfect politician's wife—she knew how to entertain. She wasn't a country bumpkin like myself."

"You aren't a country bumpkin. You have wonderful manners and I'm so happy that you are here with us to help teach my children to grow up to be ladies and gentlemen. It's up to you if you want to go. Sounds like the Senator could use your company."

"Let me think about it. He has a big house and servants. Would be a nice vacation."

Telephones had recently come to some parts of the area, but not to Daisy's farm. Aunt Lillie Fern asked Daisy to take her to Allred's store so she could use the phone there to call the Senator. She tried not to let the men sitting around in the store know who she was calling collect. Daisy tried to engage them in conversation about their crops to distract them from Lillie's conversation. She didn't hear what Lillie Fern was saying.

On the way home, Lillie told Daisy that Senator B. sounded so pitiful that she told him she would come. He insisted on sending her the train ticket. She would be leaving the following week on Tuesday.

"I think that is the right thing for you to do, Aunt Lillie."

"I hope those men in the store didn't hear my conversation. Most of them are such gossips. They will tell it all over the county that I am going to Washington to visit a widower."

The next few days were busy ones for the Pate household. There were green beans to can, blackberries to pick and make jelly. Lillie Fern got out every piece of summer clothing from the chiffarobe in her bedroom.

"I do wish I had a new frock and hat," she said to Daisy. "My older ones are getting out of style, I've had them so long."

"I'll take you to town on Saturday and see if you can find something. I think Efirds is having a summer sale. I haven't seen you so excited and enthusiastic about anything since you came here."

"You are so busy, Daisy. I could wait until I get to Washington to go shopping. I do wish I had learned to drive when I was younger. Living in a city, I never had any use for an automobile. I used to be able to drive a horse and buggy. I could ride a horse quite well when I was growing up." Charlie Jones delivered another letter from Washington. It was marked "Special Delivery."

"You are goin' to have to sign for this one, Miss Lillie Fern," Charlie said. "Must be mighty important. I hear tell you made a phone call to Washington, D.C. the other day."

"Yes, I did. I still have several friends there. After all, I lived there nearly 50 years."

On Tuesday morning the whole family got up early and got their chores done so they could accompany Aunt Lillie Fern to the train station.

"I feel like she is going away forever," said Billy Joe. "I will really miss her good biscuits and cornbread, and I'll miss her, too."

The train pulled away and all four of them waved and threw kisses as the white- gloved hand waved back.

"Aunt Lillie Fern looks so pretty in her new white hat. I hope I'm as pretty as she is when I'm her age," mused Lizzy.

"You'll never be that pretty or cook as good," teased Billy Joe.

Almost a week passed before a letter arrived from Lillie Fern. Charlie Jones delivered it to Daisy.

"Here's a letter from Lillie Fern. Hope she is havin' a good time in Washington."

"Thank you, Charlie."

"Well, ain't you goin' to open it?"

"I'll wait until supper time and read it to the family when we are all together."

"Oh! Guess I'd better go along and finish my mail route."

When everyone was at the table before the blessing was said, Daisy announced, "We have a letter from Aunt Lillie Fern."

Everyone got quiet as Daisy read,

Dear Ones,

I arrived in Washington and was met by the Senator's butler. He drove me to the Senator's home. It is so beautiful. I have my own room and my very own bathroom. Wish you could see it. Everything matches. The Senator's late wife had a real knack for decorating. I'm really having a good time. I've been to two dinner parties with the Senator and he has had one here at his house. We attended the opera one evening and we went to his church last Sunday. I could almost get used to this kind of life! I hope all is going well there on the farm. I will write again when I have time. I still do not know how long I will stay.

Love to all, Lillie Fern

"Sounds like she really is having a wonderful vacation. I'm afraid she will never want to come back here," Mary Lou said.

"She'll be back, don't you worry your pretty head about it," Daisy smiled as she envisioned that beautiful house and all the luxuries that Lillie Fern was experiencing.

Another week passed and Mr. Jones brought a letter postmarked "Washington, D.C."

"How's Lillie Fern likin' bein' in the big city?" he drawled.

"She's having a good time, and I'm sure she'll be coming home one of these days."

"Tell her next time you write to her that I miss her and I hope she comes home soon. You know, I've knowed her all my life, went to school with her. I thought she was the prettiest gal in our class; in fact, in our whole school. If'n she hadna' gone off to work in Washington I might have asked her to marry me." He laughed and spit a stream of tobacco juice that almost hit Daisy's feet.

Daisy could not wait to read the letter.

Dear Ones,

I am still having a marvelous time, seeing old friends and having long talks with the Senator. Everyone says his health is so much better since I am here. He has been so lonely and depressed since his wife died. She was a wonderful woman and he loved her very much. Now, he says he must move on. He wants me to be part of his life. I am so torn between staying here and returning home. I feel like he needs me and

I feel like all of you need me. I am praying that I make the right decision. He has asked me to marry him. It is hard for me to believe that I can have romance in my life at this age. I suppose secretly I have always been in love with him. I have always admired him as a person and for his political position. I would like to know your opinion of this situation and I need your help to make this decision that will affect all our lives. I love each of you dearly and have been perfectly happy and content living with you. Please pray for me and write me your thoughts of what I should do.

Love to all, Aunt Lillie Fern

"My, my, my," Daisy said out loud. "As much as I need her, we all need her, I want her to be happy. Just wait until I read this to the children."

After supper, Daisy gathered the children around and read the letter to them.

"I knew it," Billy Joe said. "I knew she would never come back."

"I think it is so romantic," said Lizzy. "It's just like in some of the books I've been reading."

"Reminds me of Cinderella," Mary Lou chimed in.

"What do you think, Adam?" Daisy asked.

"Well, I'm happy for her, but I surely will miss all her good cooking, especially her chocolate cakes and sugar cookies. Mother, what do you think?"

"I'm like Lizzy. I think it is so romantic. It is wonderful for Aunt Lillie Fern to have someone who cares for her and wants to take care of her in her senior years."

"You mean her old age?" Billy Joe said.

"At your age anyone over 40 seems old."

"Not really. Some of the best baseball players are over 40," he retorted.

"I'll write back and give her our blessing. Would be nice if each of you wrote a note to her, telling her you are happy for her and the Senator."

"Just think, we'll have a former Senator in our family," Adam mused.

Aunt Lillie Fern sent train tickets for Daisy and the family so they could go to the wedding. It was held at the Senator's church with lots of fanfare. She even bought Daisy and the girls new outfits and new suits for the boys.

Lillie and the Senator left on a motor trip to Florida for their honeymoon.

Daisy and the children returned to the farm, to their routine of gathering in the crops and getting ready for school to start.

Billy Joe was listening to a baseball game on Aunt Lillie Fern's radio when suddenly a news report broke in on the game. The reporter said, "It is with great sadness that I report the death of former Senator Beauregard Calhoun. He died with a heart attack just after his return from his honeymoon. Our condolences go out to his bride—Lillie Fern."

Aunt Lillie Fern returned from Washington after the Senator's funeral. His driver brought her in a big black Packard car.

The children were all fascinated by the Packard. The driver, a very personable young man, allowed them to climb all over it and even showed the huge motor to the boys. Anthony was his name. He spent the night with them. The following day Daisy and the children accompanied Aunt Lillie Fern in the Packard to the Brightwood Baptist Church in Leesburg where a graveside service was held for the Senator. He was laid to rest beside his first wife.

There were many people from all over the State shaking hands with Lillie Fern and extending their sympathy. Since the Senator had served in World War I and was a national representative, there was a military escort. A bugler played taps and the soldiers fired a 21-gun salute. The children had never seen anything like it before and they stood wide-eyed, taking it all in.

It took about two hours to drive back to the farm. Although the children felt badly for Lillie Fern, they really enjoyed the ride in the big comfortable automobile and seeing some of the State that they had never seen before.

"Just wait until school starts and I can tell that snooty Louise Smith that I rode in a big fine Packard car," Mary Lou whispered to Elizabeth.

They arrived home and it was time to take off their Sunday-best clothes and do the farm chores. Anthony spent another night with them. Being a city fellow, he enjoyed following the Pates around as they did their farm chores. He left early the next morning to drive the Packard back to Washington.

Lillie Fern was very quiet and spent most of her time in her room for the next few days. On Sunday she got dressed in one of her black dresses, put on a black hat and went to church. There were hugs and much attention paid to her.

The following week a letter came for Lillie Fern. It came special delivery and, of course, the mailman was curious to know whom it was from. Lillie Fern signed for it, but would not satisfy his curiosity. She opened it after he was gone. To her surprise it was from Senator Calhoun's lawyer in Washington.

Dear Mrs. Calhoun,

Please accept my deepest sympathy in the passing of your husband.

He was a wonderful client and friend. I am his power of attorney and I have read his will before the clerk of court and I would like to come to visit you in your home. I know you are grieving at this time, but there are some matters that need to be taken care of as soon as possible. I'm enclosing my card and phone number. Please call me to arrange our meeting.

Sincerely,
Jonathan R. Craven, JJ.D

Lillie Fern showed the letter to Daisy. "What would be a good time for him to come?" she asked.

"I think Friday," Daisy replied. "I'll go to the store and use their phone and call him to make the arrangements. I'll be glad when the phone lines finally come into this part of the county."

Friday came and everyone was up early and completed their chores. Lillie Fern had made one of her famous pound cakes and a big pitcher of lemonade.

At 10:00 o'clock an automobile came up the driveway and a man in a navy blue suit, white shirt and dark tie carrying a briefcase knocked on the door.

Lillie Fern opened the door. He said, "Mrs. Calhoun? I'm Jonathan Craven."

"Yes, I'm Lillie Fern Calhoun. Please come in. I think we met in the Senator's office when you first became his lawyer."

"I do recall meeting you, so good to see you again." He warmly shook her hand, "Senator Calhoun said you were the best secretary that anyone could ever have."

"Thank you for telling me. He was the best person to work for. I was very fortunate to be part of his team. Then to have had the privilege of being his wife, even for a short time, was more than I ever dreamed."

Opening his brief case, he said, "Mrs. Calhoun, the Senator has provided for you in his will. He has left a trust for you that will give you an income of $100.00 per month as long as you live; also the Packard automobile and all the furniture in the house in Washington."

Lillie Fern let out a gasp at the same time tears welled in her eyes. "I don't know what to say, that dear man, he was a kind person when he was alive and his kindness has not stopped with his death."

"Perhaps you can come to Washington and decide what to do with all that furniture. If you don't want to move it here I'm sure you can sell it. My office will help you in anyway that we can."

"Thank you so much, Mr. Craven. I just cannot believe this is happening."

"Mrs. Calhoun, the house has been given to the Washington, D.C. historical society to be used as a tourist attraction. You might recall that the Senator bought it from the descendants of a very prominent Washington family. It is a very old house."

"Oh! But it was very modern with indoor plumbing and a heating and lighting system that was very modern."

"Yes, the Senator had it renovated several years ago to make it more comfortable for the first Mrs. Calhoun."

"I really liked their modern kitchen, everything was so convenient. Speaking of a kitchen, I made a pound cake and lemonade. May I serve you some?"

"Yes, ma'am, that sounds so good. I haven't had homemade pound cake since I was home last Easter."

"Where is home?" she asked.

"Columbia, South Carolina. I go back there for most holidays. My wife is from there, too. We were high school sweethearts. We have three children. This cake and lemonade are delicious. Thank you very much. Nothing like Southern hospitality. I have some papers for you to sign, and then I'll be on my way. I have a long drive back. We can arrange to have the Packard delivered to you."

"That will be wonderful. I don't drive but my niece drives. I am truly blessed."

They said their goodbyes and as soon as Mr. Craven was out the door the children burst into the room. All talking at once —"Aunt Lillie Fern, you are rich, you will have the biggest car in the county, we're so glad that you are our Aunt and that you live with us."

"Calm down, children," Daisy commanded. "Remember, Aunt Lillie hasn't gotten over the shock of losing her husband and now all this." She put her arms around Lillie who was sobbing.

Through her tears she said, "Thank you God for being so good to me and my dear ones."

CHAPTER 12

Early one morning in June, Bo knocked on the back screen door while Daisy, Aunt Lillie Fern and the children were eating breakfast.

"Miz Pate, excuse me, please, but I'd like to talk to you 'bout somethin'."

"Come on in, Bo. Would you like some breakfast?"

"No, ma'am, I's already eat."

"How about a cup of coffee?"

"No, ma'am."

Daisy stepped out onto the back porch. "You sound so serious, Bo, what is it?"

"It is serious, ma'am. I wants to git married and that's serious," he grinned, showing white teeth as his eyes lit up. "You know I've been fixin' up yo tenant house an it's right livable. My girlfriend, Nettie Mae, and me has been writin to each other ever since I went home at Christmas. I's asked her to marry me and she said yes."

"Why, Bo, I think that is marvelous."

"I knows I'm not really good enough for her, she's more educated than I is. But she can teach me a lot of things. She's a school teacher. Reckon she can git a job at the colored school over in Franklin?"

"She might be able to do that. Where is the wedding going to be and when is the big day?"

"Miz Pate, that's what I wanted to talk to you about. I'd need a few days off."

"This is a busy time of year here on the farm, Bo. Why don't you have Nettie Mae to come here and you could get married. Aunt Lillie's flower garden would be a beautiful place for a wedding. Our front yard is looking good and we could get some chairs from the church."

"Hold on, Miz Pate. Don't you remember that we is colored folks and you is white? What would yo neighbors say 'bout you having a Negro wedding in yo's yard?"

"Don't worry about that, Bo. I'm a Quaker. We Quakers have always treated people of other races fairly. Haven't you heard about the underground railroad that was used during slavery days to rescue Negroes? Quakers had a lot to do with that. My great grandma hid runaway slaves during the Civil War. My grandpa used to tell us stories about what his mother did and we were so proud of her."

"Nettie Mae's daddy is a preacher. She wants him to marry us."

"Her family and friends could all come here. I'll write them a letter and invite them."

"That's mighty nice of you, Miz Pate. I just don't want to cause you any trouble. You've been so good to me."

"Bo, you've been such good help to me. I don't think I could have kept this farm going if you had not come along to help me. Now give me Nettie Mae's address so I can write her a letter." Daisy got some paper and a pen and wrote it down.

"Mama, what did Bo want?" Billy Joe asked.

"He wants to get married," Daisy replied.

"Get married?" all four children echoed.

"Who is he going to marry?" Aunt Lillie asked.

"Her name is Nettie Mae."

"Where is the wedding going to be; can we go?" asked Elizabeth.

"Well," Daisy began, "I told him we could have the wedding right here in Aunt Lillie Fern's flower garden. That is if Nettie Mae wants to have it here. I'm going to write her a letter and ask her."

"A wedding. I love weddings," Mary Lou chimed in.

The children scattered to do their chores. Aunt Lillie Fern began to clear the dishes.

"Daisy, I wasn't going to say anything in front of the children, but what are you doing, inviting Negroes to have a wedding in your yard?"

"I don't see anything wrong with it.

"You don't, and I don't, but what will all our neighbors say and think? You know how folks like to talk."

"Well, let them. Bo is a good person and I'm sure he wouldn't marry anyone that wasn't just as nice."

"That's not what I am talking about. I'm sure they are nice people, but you know how people are when it comes to white folks and colored folks socializing."

"I wouldn't call a wedding of two good people who are in love socializing. Her father is a preacher and he will be the one to perform the ceremony. I'm sure they will want to bring some of their family and friends with them."

"Never mind, you are too good, Daisy, for your own good. You think with your heart instead of your brain."

Daisy wrote a letter to Nettie Mae, inviting her to have the wedding in her yard. Nettie Mae wrote back that after talking it over with her parents they had approved. The day the letter arrived, Charlie Jones, the mailman, being nosy as usual, said to Daisy, "I see you got a letter from the gal that usually writes to your hired hand, Bo. You must be getting' chummy with all them colored folks."

Daisy felt like saying "None of your business," but she replied, "They are all nice folks."

"I reckon they are. That Bo sure is a hard worker. I hear he's been fixin' up your tenant house. I drove over by it one day and it's lookin' good. He's even got the yard lookin' good."

"Yes, he's made it livable again. The house had gotten run down after Grandfather died."

Charlie drove away.

Daisy looked around the yard and the rose garden and imagined how the wedding would be. Nettie Mae had set Saturday afternoon at 2:00 on June 30th for the wedding. The mailman kept tabs on the letters being exchanged between Daisy and Nettie Mae. Curiosity finally got the best of him and he asked Daisy what was going on between her and those colored folks.

Daisy told him about the wedding.

On Wednesday night before the wedding, Daisy and the family had been to prayer meeting at their church. They had gone to bed right after they got home. It was a warm night and all the bedroom windows were open.

Suddenly Daisy heard a noise that sounded like horses' hooves on the gravel driveway. She lay there for a few minutes thinking she had dreamed it. She decided to look out the window. Pulling back the curtain, she saw something bright light up the front yard. She ran into Aunt Lillie Fern's room and said in a loud whisper, "Get up; there is something going on in our yard."

Lillie jumped up and ran to the window with Daisy. They could not believe what they were seeing!

There on the lawn near the flower garden was a cross that was blazing and surrounding it were eight figures in white robes, their faces covered with only holes for their eyes and mouths. They were not saying a word.

"Shall I get the shotgun?" Lillie whispered to Daisy.

"No, don't do that. They will be gone in a minute. I hope the children don't wake up."

"I wish I knew their names. They are a bunch of cowards who keep their faces covered. You know why they did this, Daisy. They found out about the wedding."

"That Charlie Jones," he must have told them. Who knows, he might be one of the KKK."

The men mounted their horses and rode away. As soon as they were gone, Daisy slipped on her shoes, grabbed a bucket of water and threw it on the burning cross. As soon as the fire was out, she pushed it over and when it was cool enough she dragged it to the woodshed. "I'll chop it up in the morning before the children get up. I don't want the children or Bo to see it. It's hard for me to believe that people can have so much hate in their hearts that they would do anything so evil."

The next morning, Daisy went to the woodshed before everyone got up and chopped what was left of the cross into kindling wood. She went into the yard and with a rake fixed the grass where the cross had been driven into the ground. She went into the flower garden, got on her knees and prayed, "Lord, forgive me for the bad thoughts I am having about those men. I ask you to make them see the errors of their ways. Amen."

Aunt Lillie Fern baked two of her most delicious pound cakes and designed a wedding cake out of them. She made white icing and on the day of the wedding decorated it with fresh flowers from her garden. She had pressed the best white linen tablecloth and placed it on the dining room table. With the help of Lizzy and Mary Lou she had made pimiento and cheese sandwiches and dainty biscuits with pieces of thinly cut fried ham.

"Everything looks so pretty, Aunt Lillie Fern," Lizzy said.

"Couldn't have done it without you and Mary Lou's help."

Four cars and three buggies loaded with colored people began to arrive. Adam and Billy Joe were directing them as to where they should park.

Nettie Mae and her parents knocked on the front door. Daisy invited them in. Nettie Mae was dressed in a beautiful white suit, white hat, white gloves and white shoes. Since they had never met, they introduced themselves. Nettie's Mother was dressed in a navy blue suit with matching accessories. Her Father had on a black suit, white shirt with a clergy collar. He held a black hat in his hand and a Bible under his arm.

Aunt Lillie Fern has made a red rose corsage for you and it will look so pretty on your beautiful white suit. She made Bo a boutonnière. Speaking of Bo, I told him he must not see you before the ceremony, that it was bad luck." She noticed a frown come across the preacher's forehead. "Of course, we don't believe in luck, but that is just an old saying that someone told me when I got married. So, Nettie Mae, you stay here in the parlor until it is time for the wedding."

"We brought a piano on a truck and the men are unloading it now. The pianist at my church will be playing it for the wedding," Nettie's father spoke in a booming voice. I'll go out and help them get ready."

A lady in a pink flowered dress and pink flowered hat began to play the piano at 15 minutes to 2:00. All the people were seated in the chairs that had been set up in the yard.

Bo was all dressed up in a new navy blue suit, white shirt and black bow tie. His shoes were so shiny Billy Joe thought he could see himself in them.

Bo walked up to Daisy's front door as Nettie Mae stepped out. She took his arm and they walked into the yard between the chairs as the pianist played, "Here Comes the Bride." They stood under the arch of the trellis where Aunt Lillie Fern's pink roses were blooming. Nettie's father read some passages from the Bible about marriage, prayed and then had Nettie Mae and Bo exchange their vows. He pronounced them husband and wife and allowed the groom to kiss his bride.

Daisy invited everyone to come into the house for the reception.

At first, some of the colored people hesitated to come into the house, especially through the front door. They soon felt at ease with Daisy and her family. They complimented Aunt Lillie on the beautiful cake, food and lemonade.

Bo was nervous when he and Nettie Mae were cutting the cake. Some people were making pictures as they had done at the wedding in the yard. Bo, in a trembling voice, said," I want to thank all of you for comin' today and I wants to thank Miz Pate, Miz Lillie and all the children for givin' me a place to work and a place to live. I think most of you all know that Miz Pate saved my life when I had been hurt. These are good folks and they live and work everyday like everybody should do. I can never thank you enough for what you have dun fo' me. God bless you."

Bo's brother, J.T., spoke up, "Now, we all want to see yo' house and where yo' bride is gonna have to put up with you."

"The trunk of our car is full of weddin' presents and we want to put them in your house," Nettie's father said. Nettie Mae's brother brought her car, a yellow 1932 Chevrolet roadster with a rumble seat, from where he had hid it behind the woodshed. However, Billy Joe, Adam and some other boys knew where it was and had tied some old tin cans and old shoes onto the back bumper. The cans made a lot of noise on the dirt road.

Nettie told Bo to drive as he helped her into the front seat. Her parents followed in their car, but all the others walked behind to go see where Bo and Nettie would live.

Daisy and Lillie stayed behind to clean up the dishes.

"Everything really went well," Daisy said, as she breathed a sigh of relief.

Someone knocked at the back door. Daisy opened it and there stood Thomas Ferrell in his sheriff's uniform.

"I'm just checking by to see if everything is all right. I heard there was goin' to be a weddin' here today," he drawled. "I see there are lots of cars and buggies around."

"Come in, Thomas, and have some wedding cake and lemonade."

"Don't mind if I do. Where's all the colored folks?"

"They have gone over to see where Bo and his bride are going to live."

"I have to hand it to you, Daisy, you and Miz Lillie do beat all lookin' after other folks. I wish I had your nerve."

"We just try to live by what the good book says, and treat our fellowman with love and respect," Aunt Lillie said as she cut Thomas a piece of cake.

"I heard there was a cross burnin' out here the other night."

"Who told you that, Thomas? I haven't told a living soul, not even my children."

"Word gets around, Daisy. That's why I came today, to make sure there wouldn't be any trouble."

"No trouble at all, Thomas. I'd appreciate it if you'd be on your way before the folks get back here to their cars to go home. You know how the sight of the law scares some people."

"Well, I'll be on my way then. Thanks for that good cake and lemonade, Miz Lillie."

After he was gone, Daisy said, "Some people just try to stir up trouble. Can't even have a wedding without somebody sticking their nose in where it don't belong."

Chapter 13

"Mama, Mama," Adam shouted excitedly as he burst through the kitchen door.

"What is it?" asked Daisy.

"Can we go to the county fair and let me take my prize rooster to show? I might win a blue ribbon, he's such a fine big rooster, and you know how he struts all around the barnyard."

"Slow down, Adam."

"Mr. Reynolds, the County Agent from the Agriculture Office, came to our school today. He took all of us boys aside and told us how we should enter the county fair and show off what we are raising. He also told us about the canning and baking bread and pies and cakes contests that they have at the fair. You and Aunt Lillie Fern should enter. He even gave me an application to fill out."

"When is the fair?"

"Next month, October 10th through 17th. Please say we can go."

"I suppose you would have to take your rooster and leave him there all week."

"Mr. Reynolds said we could do that. Said to bring plenty of food for him. I would have to be there on the day of the judging."

"Adam, I have never seen you so excited over anything."

"Mama, I am excited. I've never been to the fair. I know they have rides like the Ferris wheel and Bubba Jones told me they have sideshows. Said he saw a bearded lady and a man who was half man and half alligator."

"Perhaps this is the year we can go. Let's not tell the other children until we know definitely that we are going. Since we have the automobile that Aunt Lillie Fern inherited from the Senator, we can travel comfortably. I'm not sure that our old truck could make it to the fair. I'll write and get some more information about entering the baking and canning contests."

"In the meantime, I'll get my rooster groomed for the contest," Adam said as he went out to find the rooster he had named Ben Franklin.

The day finally came when Adam had to take Ben Franklin to the fair. With the help of Bo, he had built a nice wire coop in which to carry him. Aunt Lillie Fern had baked one of her prize pound cakes to enter and Daisy was entering a jar of pickled peaches and one of blackberry jelly. The two women were almost as excited as Adam. They arrived at the fairgrounds and were ushered through the gates with special passes. They found the places where they displayed their goods. The judging would take place before noon and then the fair would be opened to the public.

"We will stay until the judging," Daisy said, "Then we have to go home. We will come back one day and bring Billy Joe, Lizzy and Mary Lou. If Bo can handle the evening chores, we can stay until after dark when they have the fireworks. That was my favorite part of the fair when I was a child."

Daisy and Lillie Fern walked around looking at all the flower and food displays. Also, the quilts and fancy handwork entered by the women of the county.

Adam stayed close to Ben Franklin, keeping an eye on the other poultry that had been entered. "I think you are the most beautiful rooster here, Ben Franklin."

The judges came by stopping to feel the legs and feathers and admiring the tail feathers and combs of each rooster.

Adam was afraid that Ben Franklin would peck one of the judges. He strutted around in his cage like he knew that he had to put on a show and even threw his head back and let out a loud crow.

The judges went to the end of the cages and stood whispering to one another and looking at the cards where they had been making notes. One man stepped forward with a blue ribbon in his hand.

Adam was holding his breath.

He came right up to Ben Franklin's cage and pinned a blue ribbon on it. He read the card attached to the cage, "Ben Franklin, owner Adam Pate." "Congratulations, Adam, for first place. This is a mighty fine rooster."

"Thank you, sir. I think he is beautiful."

The judges went on down the line of cages pinning ribbons.

Daisy and Aunt Lillie Fern came to Adam. "Your rooster won, congratulations, Adam," his mother spoke excitedly. Aunt Lillie Fern won a blue ribbon for her cake and I won two red ones for my canned goods."

Friday was the day that all school age children got into the fair free of charge. School let out at noon and as soon as the children got home they all jumped into the big black car and were on their way. Aunt Lillie Fern sat in the front seat with Daisy and the excited four children in the back seat.

"Mother," Mary Lou said above the excited voices of the children, "I was talking to Alice Brown today and telling her that we were going to the fair. She burst into tears and said I wish I could go, I've never been. Remember last year when her mother died we went to their house and took some food?"

"Yes, honey, I remember her," Daisy answered.

"Mother, I feel so sorry for her. She is always crying at school. I wish we could take her to the fair with us."

"Mary Lou, that is a good idea. We will pass right by her house, we can stop and see if her Dad will let her go."

"Where will she sit?" asked Billy Joe. "I don't want to sit by a girl."

"Billy Joe, if you feel that way, you will have to come sit in front between Aunt Lillie and me."

"Yes, ma'am."

They stopped at Alice Brown's house and Mary Lou went up to knock at the door. A man in dirty overalls looking as if he had not shaved in several days opened the door and stepped onto the porch.

"What you want!" he said, slurring his words.

"I was wondering if Alice could go to the fair with us," Mary Lou said in a shy voice.

"Alice, come out here," Mr. Brown shouted.

A frightened looking girl appeared at the door. She smiled when she saw Mary Lou.

"She wants you to go to the fair with them."

"Can I, Papa, can I?" Alice begged.

"Well, I reckon you can, but we ain't got no money to spend on sech foolish things."

"School children get in free today."

Daisy got out of the car and assured Mr. Brown that she would take good care of Alice. She smelled alcohol.

"It will be sort of late when we get home as we plan to stay for the fireworks. Would it be all right for Alice to come home with us and spend the night?"

"That's all right with me, just so she gets home in time to do her Saturday chores. You know my wife died last year and Alice has a lot of work to do to help me keep this place going. Mighty fine looking automobile you got there. I hear tell yo Aunt inherited it from that old Senator man. It pays off to know the right people!" he laughed and spat a stream of tobacco juice out into the yard. "Maybe you'll take me fer a ride sometime."

Daisy didn't answer him but told Alice to bring a sweater, as it would get cold after the sun goes down.

Alice came out with a worn pink sweater. "My Mama knitted this for me before she died and I just love it," she said as she got into the back seat with Mary Lou, Lizzy and Adam. "Bye, Papa. Thanks for letting me go."

Aunt Lillie Fern opened her purse just before they arrived at the parking lot of the fair. "I'm giving each of you children a dollar to spend at the fair and that includes you, too, Alice."

"That is kind of you," said Alice. "But I don't need any money." She pulled out a small change purse from a pocket on her dress. "See, I have some money that Papa doesn't know about. Some men come to our house to play cards with Papa and I make coffee and sometimes molasses cookies and serve to them. When Papa isn't looking, they slip me a quarter or a dime and I save it to buy things I want. Papa doesn't have much money unless he wins some when the men play cards and he has to use that for groceries and tobacco to chew and when he comes in carrying a brown bag I know he is going to drink what's in it. Papa is so funny when he drinks. He sings and plays his fiddle and gets me to dance."

Aunt Lillie Fern couldn't help but roll her eyes at Daisy as Alice chatted on about her life.

"Do you have any brothers or sisters?" Lillie Fern asked.

"I have one brother, but he left home and joined the Navy. He's on a big ship somewhere near China. He said he didn't want to be a farmer like Papa."

"What's wrong with being a farmer?" Adam chimed in. "That's what I want to be."

"Nothing, I don't guess, but Jim said he didn't want to make a living scratching out of the ground. He wanted to see the world. That's why he joined the Navy. He has gone to all sorts of new places. I wish some day I could go there, too," Alice replied wistfully.

They all went through the gate at the fair, the children getting in free. Adam and Billy Joe left them to go check on Ben Franklin and promised to meet them at the arena at 8:00 to watch the fireworks. "Don't go in any of those sideshows," Daisy warned. The girls walked around with Daisy and Lillie Fern. They stopped and let the girls ride the hobbyhorses while they sat on a bench and ate cotton candy. When they came to the Ferris wheel, Daisy said, "Aunt Lillie, if you don't mind sitting here alone, I'd like to ride. It's been years since I've been on one."

Daisy and Lizzy got in one seat and Mary Lou and Alice in another. Up, up they went, all four were screaming. Daisy and Lizzy stopped on top and clung to each other as the seat swung back and forth. Daisy remembered how it had felt the first time she rode a Ferris wheel. It was when she was sixteen and she had a date for the fair with Thomas Ferrell. She remembered what fun they had sitting close together and scared to death as the seat swung back and forth.

"Mommy, are you scared?" Lizzy asked.

"Are you, Lizzy?"

"Yes, ma'am, but I'm glad you are here to hug me."

"I was just remembering the first time that I ever rode a Ferris wheel. It was with a boy."

"I hope my first date will be going to the fair."

"Well, you have a few years to look forward to that," Daisy laughed and squeezed Lizzy even closer."

All seven of them met at the arena to watch the fireworks.

Billy Joe had won a brown teddy bear for throwing baseballs to knock over milk bottles. Adam had won a plastic monkey that ran up and down a stick when he pulled his string for picking up the right duck at the booth where little wooden ducks with numbers painted on them floated in water. Everyone had eaten hotdogs and cotton candy.

When they arrived home everyone fell into bed exhausted.

After breakfast and before the chores started, Daisy, along with Mary Lou, took Alice home. On the way Daisy asked, "Alice, do you go to Sunday School?"

"No, ma'am, not since Mama died. She used to take me but Papa doesn't think it's necessary to go to church. He says if God cared about us, he would not have made Mama die. He is so sad without her. I think that is why he drinks that old liquor."

"Honey, God didn't make your Mother die. He just needed another angel in Heaven to help Him. I went to school with your Mother. She was so sweet and pretty and you are just like her."

"Thank you, everyone says I look like her, especially my Grandmother Smith."

"Do you get to see your Grandparents often?"

"No, Papa won't let me go to their house except at Christmas. Won't even let me go for Thanksgiving. Grandma is such a good cook and I love to eat her food. Papa and I aren't very good cooks. When I went at Christmas, Grandma loaded me up food—all kinds of good cake and pie, ham, chicken and dressing and biscuits. She can make the best biscuits. I hope I can learn to make them. She and Grandfather give me lots of gifts at Christmas.

They send me clothes and things in the mail, especially for my birthday. I wish I could see them more often. I like their house. It is big and they have a piano. My Mama used to play it when she was a little girl."

Daisy, with a lump in her throat, said, "Perhaps your Father will let you spend a Saturday night with Mary Lou soon and you can go to Sunday School and Church with us.

"Oh! Could I?" I'd love that. Thank you for taking me to the fair." She skipped up the steps to her house and turned and waved goodbye.

Daisy choked back tears.

Mary Lou spoke in a trembling voice, "I feel so sorry for her because she doesn't have a good mother like I have. Mommy, I love you."

"I love you, too, Mary Lou. I hope we can do something to help her. I might go pay a visit to the Smiths. I know where they live as I went to parties at their home when I was in high school.

Sunday morning brought crispness in the air, reminding everyone of fall. The leaves on the trees of the farm were bright orange, yellow and red.

Daisy, Aunt Lillie Fern and the children hurried to do their chores and arrived at Sunday School on time. Between Sunday School and the preaching service, Mamie Singletary accosted Daisy and Lillie. Mamie, in her plain brown dress and the same brown hat that she had worn for years, said, "Daisy and Lillie Fern, I heard that you all went to the fair. Don't you know that good Quakers don't go to such places? Why, I heard that they have sideshows with half-naked women and men prancing around in them. And you, Lillie Fern, a Sunday School teacher! I guess you learned those worldly ways when you lived in Washington. You wear lipstick and even dye your hair." She stopped to take a breath.

Daisy said, "Mamie, yes, we did go to the fair. Adam won a blue ribbon for his pet rooster and Lillie won a blue ribbon for her pound cake. You've always said she was the best pound cake baker in this church."

Mamie continued with her diatribe, "Also heard that you took that good-for-nothing Clyde Brown's daughter Alice with you. Poor child, lost her mother last year and Clyde drinks and don't halfway take care of her. I never could understand why a nice girl like Ruby Mae Smith with her upbringing married that Clyde Brown. You know he never would let her have anything to do with her folks after they married. I heard that she died because he wouldn't let her go to the doctor. Said he claimed he didn't have the money."

Daisy replied, "Mamie, Ruby Mae died from pneumonia. She died in the hospital. Her husband and daughter are very upset over her passing. I don't think we should be talking about them. Alice is very sweet child and one of Mary Lou's friends."

The church bell rang summoning them to go in.

Lillie whispered to Daisy," Mamie thinks going to the fair is a sin, but she never has considered that gossiping is also a sin. Besides I do not dye my hair; I just don't have many gray ones like she does."

CHAPTER 14

Daisy often thought of how she was blessed to have four well-behaved children. They excelled in school and each had chores to do on the farm, and seldom shirked their duties. Their father would have been very proud of them. Sometimes they traded jobs with one another and competed to see who accomplished the most in the shortest length of time. All learned to milk the cow.

Mary Lou's favorite job was to feed the chickens and gather the eggs. At times she was afraid of Ben Franklin, the rooster, who won the prize at the fair. It seemed he realized that he was special, the way he strutted around the fenced-in chicken yard. She would throw shelled corn as far away as she could from the door of the hen house so he would be occupied while she went in to gather the eggs.

Elizabeth liked to milk Bossie. She was a gentle cow and dutifully came to the barn from the pasture every evening. She also liked to churn the butter. It was fun to her to gather the butter out of the wooden churn and work it with her hands until all the milk was out of it, then place a blob of it into the wooden mold and carefully push the top down and out would come a square of butter ready to be spread on hot biscuits or to be used in Aunt Lillie Fern's pound cakes. Elizabeth was learning to cook and had won a prize in the Home Economics class, using her Great Aunt's pound cake recipe.

Billy Joe's favorite duty was to climb into the barn loft and pitch the hay down to feed the animals. He called himself the water boy because he carried water from the well for the chickens. He took turns with Adam to mix the hog slop with table scraps, leftover milk and wheat bran to feed the hog that would provide meat for the winter. They tried not to get too attached to the pig, because it would be sad to eat a pet.

Adam had learned to plow with the two mules, Maud and Kate. Bo had taught him to use the turning plow to plow a straight furrow, then to sit on the hard cold metal seat of the harrow to break the big clods until the ground was smooth enough for planting. His favorite season was planting time. To watch the seeds coming up was to him an amazing sight. Wheat and rye were planted in late fall or early January, corn and cotton in spring.

Most Quaker farmers in the area did not plant tobacco as they considered it was sinful to smoke cigarettes or cigars, chew tobacco or dip snuff.

The spring of 1939 was an exciting one for the Pates. Adam was graduating from high school. Daisy could hardly believe that her first born had completed eleven years of school. The school and church were the centers of entertainment for the rural community of Pleasant Grove. High school graduation provided nearly a week of activity every May. First was the Junior-Senior Banquet. It was held in the auditorium, which served as the basketball court, the weekly assembly, a theater for plays, and any other needs of the school or community.

Friday afternoon after school the junior class, along with several teachers and parents, worked diligently to transform the large room into the theme they had chosen for the banquet. For weeks they had painted scenery on wide boards to look like a deck of a ship for one side of the auditorium and the other side looked like the ocean with white caps on the waves and a sailboat in the distance. Most of the class had never seen the real ocean or a ship, but used their artistic skills to make it something very special. They had made other decorations for the tables out of crepe paper in the senior class colors, purple and white. Some of their mothers arranged to prepare the food. Entertainment would be some men in the community who played stringed instruments. Dancing was frowned upon in this Quaker community. Only the Virginia reel and square dancing was approved. Some of the junior class practiced with the band to perform these folk dances as part of the entertainment. Also they served the food. The girls wore white dresses with starched stiff black aprons and little black head pieces trimmed in white. The boys wore black pants, white shirts and black bow ties.

There were speeches by some of the junior class members, making cute remarks using various names of the seniors and some had written poems about them in a joking manner. The school principal and all the high school teachers were invited to speak. The president of the Senior class, none other than Adam Pate, stood up to speak.

He had been working on his appreciation speech for the junior class and the faculty for several weeks. Daisy had bought him a new suit, white shirt and tie for the occasion. The girls in the class wore evening gowns. All had corsages. Adam was allowed to drive Aunt Lillie Fern's car. He escorted Linda Mae Turner to the banquet. They had gone all eleven years to school together, but this was Adam's first real date.

A week later on Sunday afternoon the graduating class of 1939 had their baccalaureate program at the Quaker Church. The Pate family all attended. Reverend Dwight Harris of the First Baptist Church in Raleigh was the featured speaker. Before his speech, the class marched in as one of the teachers played the piano. The girls dressed in their Sunday best, all wearing hats and the boys in their suits, with their hair combed neatly, smiled as their proud parents and friends watched. They were led by the chief marshal, who was the person who had the highest average grades for their junior year. A trio of girls sang a hymn followed by a solo by a young man with a deep voice. There were speeches by the County School Superintendent, the junior class president, and by Adam, the senior class president.

Billy Joe whispered to his mother, "I'm glad I'm not a class president and would have to make all those speeches in front of everybody like Adam."

Daisy smiled at him as tears of joy ran down her face and she dabbed them with her handkerchief.

Rev. Harris spoke for nearly forty-five minutes as people fanned themselves with funeral home fans in the warm May weather. He challenged each of the class members to always do their very best and to always put God first in their lives.

After he sat down, the school principal thanked everyone for coming, made some announcements and led in prayer.

The pianist began to play "Onward Christian Soldiers," as the chief marshal led the seniors out of the church.

The following Friday night was known as Class Night. Again the junior class had been working hard to gather wild daisies from nearby fields. They used rope and carefully wove the daisies into knots in the rope to form two daisy chains. After the audience had settled in their chairs in the auditorium the junior class walked in two by two carrying the daisy chain. They stood holding them on each side of the aisle. The senior class walked in, the girls in long dresses and the boys in their suits, marched up onto the stage at the front. The junior class then carried the daisy chains and carefully laid them on the front edge of the stage.

The Salutatorian of the senior class gave the welcoming speech. The class historian read the history of the class, naming each person who started in the first grade and their teachers' names. She continued on with other information about what had happened over the past eleven years.

The class prophets read what might happen to each member of the class, all in good humor. Adam's future was foretold that he would head the Agriculture Department of the whole United States.

Awards were given for academic achievements and sports achievements by the principal. Each class member received an award for something, including the persons who drove the school buses. The Valedictorian gave the closing speech.

The Junior class picked up the daisy chains and held them along the aisle as the Seniors walked off the stage and to the back of the auditorium waving and smiling at their parents and friends.

The next day was the big one! Aunt Lillie Fern had ordered Lizzy and Mary Lou each a dress from the Montgomery Ward

Catalog and Billy Joe a pair of navy blue pants and a blue shirt. She had kept it a secret until the day before graduation. Lizzy had asked her mother what could she wear and Daisy had not wanted to give away the surprise. The dresses were ones that the girls had picked out of the catalog and had wished they could have. They both squealed with happiness when they came home from school and found their dresses in their room on their bed, not only dresses but a pair of white shoes for each.

Lizzy said, "I prayed that God would send me a new dress and shoes. He answered my prayer."

Mary Lou had tears in her eyes as she hugged and thanked Aunt Lillie.

Billie Joe shouted loudly when he found his pants and shirt and shoes. He ran into the girls' room to show them off and grabbed Aunt Lillie Fern and gave her a big hug. "I feel like it is Christmas in May."

Daisy was happy to see the children so pleased and thankful for the new clothes. She wondered what she would wear to Adam's graduation. She looked into the closet in her room and let out a cry of surprise! There was a blue crepe dress hanging in the middle of her closet and on her bed was a box. She opened it and carefully pulled out a white hat trimmed with blue flowers.

"Aunt Lillie, I can't believe that you did this for me! The dress and hat are beautiful. It has been so long since I've had anything new. Like Billie Joe, I feel like it is Christmas."

"I'm so thankful that I am able to give all of you something. You are so good to me, and I enjoy living here with you. There is another surprise in your closet. Look on the floor."

"Oh! Aunt Lillie, a new pair of white shoes! My old ones are so worn out. I'll be the best-dressed woman at the graduation, thanks to you!

Adam will be so proud of me. He'll be proud of his whole family."

Adam walked in, "What's all this excitement about? Oh! I see all these new clothes. Mama, I would be proud of my family if all of you were wearing gunny sacks and going barefoot!" He grabbed his mother and kissed her on the cheek.

"Aunt Lillie has ordered all these new clothes for us," Mary Lou exclaimed.

"I have a graduation present for you, Adam." Aunt Lillie gave him an envelope.

He opened it and tucked into a beautiful card was a crisp new $50.00 bill. "Aunt Lillie, "I've never seen so much money. Thank you, thank you, thank you." He kissed her on her cheek as tears came into his eyes. "Nobody has ever had an Aunt like you."

"You deserve it, Adam. You have worked so hard for a young man your age on the farm and have kept up with your grades. I am so proud of you."

"We better all get to our chores," Adams said as he went into his room to put his money into what he had always called his secret hiding place.'

Aunt Lillie said, "I must get to making a pound cake to take to the big dinner we will have after the graduation."

Commencement Day was one of the most exciting days of the school year. Many people in the community, even those without children in school, came out for the festivities. Men, women and children assembled in the auditorium in chairs that had been set up row by row. The front row seats on both aisles were reserved for the families of the graduating class. At 10:30 the sound of the piano began and the Chief Marshal led the procession down the center aisle. A preschool boy and girl, usually siblings of two of the seniors, had been chosen as mascots. The little girl dressed in her very best dress and the little boy in a suit proudly marched down the aisle followed by the seniors. The senior girls all wore white dresses and white shoes; the boys had on suits. After them came the school principal, the county superintendent of schools, the guest speaker and one of the local church pastors. The principal greeted everyone and the pastor led in prayer. The valedictorian of the class made her speech. She was Linda Mae Turner, the girl Adam had escorted to the banquet. She had made the highest grades in the class. Next came the guest speaker with an encouraging speech. Afterwards the county school superintendent called out the name of each senior and shook their hands and handed them their diploma. The principal made the announcement of the covered dish luncheon and invited everyone to stay followed by the baseball game that would be played in the afternoon and encouraged everyone to come back that night for the senior class play, "All About Nothing" at 8:00 p.m.

The senior class marched out with smiles on their faces, knowing they had accomplished a big step in their lives. There were hugs from parents and friends and words of congratulations. The ladies rushed to put their food on the long tables that had been set up under the shade of the trees in the schoolyard. There was a concession stand where ice cream, soft drinks, bananas, and other goodies could be purchased. Everything was five cents and the kind man running it often gave children who had no money whatever they wanted free.

After lunch most everyone went to the baseball field to watch the team play against another high school. Billy Joe was on the team and Daisy and Adam went to see him play while the girls spent time with their friends. Aunt Lillie visited with people she had known from her school days. Pleasant Grove won the ball game.

The Pates hurried home to feed the livestock, milk the cow, and get ready to go back to the school for the play. Adam had a part in it and had learned his lines to perfection. Daisy was so proud of her son and her thoughts were how much his father would have been also. It was times like this that she truly missed Joe and wished he could be with them.

Everyone was tired when they arrived home. Aunt Lillie and the girls went right to bed. Billy Joe was still talking about the two home runs he had at the ball game and finally went to his room to see if he could go to sleep.

Daisy and Adam sat at the kitchen table reminiscing about the events of the day. Adam asked, "Is there any way that I can go to college? I know you need me here on the farm, but I would like to go to the State Agricultural College to learn more about farming."

Daisy signed, "I do wish we had the money to send you. I know you would be a good student, but with our country going through this time of depression I do not know how we can manage it. The banks aren't loaning money these days, and we have nothing in savings."

"I know, mother. Perhaps things will get better soon. I would be willing to work and go to school too, but I know jobs are very scarce. I'll just stay here on the farm and help you and save what money I can and perhaps later on I can go to college. Don't you worry, I will read all the books I can about better ways to farm."

He kissed her goodnight and thanked her for all she had done to make his graduation a day to always remember.

CHAPTER 15

Early one morning in July, Daisy and the children got up early to get to their chores before the hot North Carolina sun would be beating down. Daisy had promised if things went well that in late afternoon they could go swimming in Mr. Frazier's pond.

"Where is Aunt Lillie?" Lizzy asked. "She is usually up before we are making biscuits."

"We better go see about here," Daisy replied. All five of them went to Lillie Fern's room. Daisy knocked on her door but she did not answer. She opened the door and tipped in, thinking that perhaps she was sleeping late.

Her eyes were closed and a sweet smile was on her lips.

"Oh! No," Daisy said excitedly.

"What's wrong?" Adam asked.

Daisy felt for a pulse on her neck. Big tears came into her eyes. "It just can't be. She has gone to Heaven to be with Jesus."

All of them started crying and leaning over her to give her a kiss, then ran out of the room, all except Daisy and Adam. They stood holding each other and the tears ran down their faces.

After a few minutes Daisy spoke, trying to gather her wits as to what should be their next move. She took the sheet on the bed and covered her beloved aunt's face. Turning to Adam, "Honey, we will have to get the doctor out here. Please get in the car and go to Mr. Berry's store and ask to use his phone to call Dr. Foxx and tell him what has happened. I'll console the other children."

She went into the kitchen and wrapped her arms around all three of them. They all stood crying. Daisy remembered how she felt when she lost Joe and her grandparents. Her heart ached not only for the children, but also for herself.

Bo knocked on the screen door of the kitchen before entering. "Where is Adam going this early in the mornin' and why are all of you cryin'?"

Mary Lou spoke sadly, "Aunt Lillie Fern has gone to be with Jesus."

"Oh! My, Oh! My," Bo said as he burst into tears. "I loved her like she was my own folks. She was always so sweet and kind to me. I'll go git Nettie Mae and our boys to come help with the chores and whatever else you need doin'."

"We must all eat our breakfast so we will have strength to do what is necessary at such a time as this," Daisy told the children.

No one was very hungry and they picked at their food.

Elizabeth said, "I'll go milk Bossie."

"I'll go feed the chickens," Mary Lou chimed in.

"I'll take care of the mules and feed the hog. Mother, with Bo's help we will take care of all the morning chores." Billy Joe hugged his mother, "You stay here in the house and wait for Dr. Foxx."

Adam returned stating that Dr. Foxx would be coming as soon as possible.

Nettie Mae came in and took over the kitchen.

Daisy went into the parlor and sat down to think of all the things that she would have to do to get ready for the funeral. Her thoughts were interrupted by a knock at the door. It was Dr. Foxx, accompanied by a young man that he introduced as a medical student that was helping him for the summer.

Daisy took them into Aunt Lillie's room. Dr. Foxx wanted to know if she knew the actual time of death.

"I do not know. She was fine when she went to bed about 9:00 last night. I do wish I had checked on her during the night. It was about 6:30 when we came in to see why she had not gotten up. There was no pulse and she felt cold to my touch," Daisy replied through her tears.

"Do not blame yourself, Daisy. It was time for God to take her home."

"I know that, but it isn't easy to give her up. She was 85 years old and I should have been expecting it to happen, but it is something we never are prepared to face."

Dr. Foxx put his arm around her. "I will get in touch with Richardson's Funeral Home and they will come out and get her. Sam Richardson will come to make the arrangements with you. You are a strong woman and I know you will get through this just as you have other things in your life. I will turn this information into the county. Let me know if you need anything. Remember you are not alone. God is with you and will comfort you."

After they left, Daisy got out a piece of paper and began to make a list of whom she should notify. "I do wish we had telephones."

Adam came in. "I wish we did, too." What can I do to help you?

"We will have to wait until Mr. Richardson gets here to make the arrangements. I'm making a list of people that we must get in touch with. Aunt Lillie always said to not make a 'big to do" over a funeral for her, but to have a celebration because she would be going to Heaven to be with her Lord and Savior, Jesus Christ. We will have a simple Quaker funeral that will honor the life of a gracious lady who loved Jesus, her family and was a friend to whomever she met."

Someone had gotten word to Pastor Adams. He arrived at Daisy's house to help console the family and help with the funeral arrangements. Mr. Richardson arrived. He brought pictures of caskets to show and discussed prices with Daisy.

"I know this is a difficult time for you all," he said. "But if I can make all the arrangements while I am here, it will save you a trip to my funeral parlor and time for both of us."

"Aunt Lillie would not want anything really elaborate, but I do want something nice."

"This one is our most popular casket and a medium price." He pointed at a picture of an off-white one. "I have one that is pink satin inside that is very appropriate for ladies. The price is $100.00 and that includes everything concerning the funeral except digging the grave and closing it. I imagine some of your neighbor men will be willing to do that for you."

"That will be a nice one for her. She has a beautiful white dressing gown that she had been saving for her burial. I'm sorry, but I will not be able to pay you until I can get the money from her insurance policy."

"That will be fine."

"When is the funeral?"

Daisy looked at Pastor Adams. Pastor Adams spoke, "This is Friday, Daisy. Don't you think Sunday afternoon at 2:00 would be a good time?"

"That will be a good time. I think we will be able to get word to all our relatives by then," Daisy nodded.

"All right, Mrs. Pate. We will have her back here to your home tomorrow afternoon around 2:00."

"I'll get the dressing gown for you. Please fix her beautiful gray hair just as she has always worn it, parted in the middle and finger waved on each side. Go lightly with the make up."

"My wife will take care of all of that. My condolence to all of your family, Mrs. Pate."

"Thank you, Mr. Richardson."

Daisy went into Aunt Lillie Fern's room alone to say a last good bye and to tell her how much she would miss her and how very much she and the children had enjoyed having her live with them and how much she loved her. She kissed her cold forehead as hot tears dripped down her face. She got the white dressing gown out of the bureau drawer and took it to Mr. Richardson.

After the hearse had gone, Daisy, the children and Pastor Adams gathered around the dining room table to plan the funeral. Daisy wanted each child to say what they wanted to have said or songs that she had loved to be used at the funeral.

"I want everyone to know what a wonderful person she was," Mary Lou said, trying to keep back tears.

"Her favorite hymn was Amazing Grace, Billy Joe sniffed as he spoke.

"The 23rd Psalm was one of her best loved chapters of the Bible," Lizzy commented. "She helped me learn it by heart when she first came to live with us. How can we live without her?" She ran from the room out into the rose garden that was Aunt Lillie Fern's pride and joy.

Adam asked, "Could I speak at the funeral? I'd like everyone to know how much she has meant to us. We don't have any grandparents to love and mentor us, but she did both for us."

Pastor Adams said, "You have all given me ideas of how the funeral should be conducted. Is there anything special that you would like to have said, Daisy?"

"Please tell everyone there how they can go to Heaven. That is what she would want."

"I'll be sure to do that. I'll be going home now. I'll be responsible to getting some men in the meeting house to dig the grave. I suppose you want it to be next to her parents in the graveyard."

"Thank you so much. Sunday afternoon at 2:00 will be the funeral and anyone who wants to come by our house Saturday afternoon and night for the viewing are welcome."

After he left Daisy turned to Adam. "We must get word to Uncle Ed in Raleigh and he can let the other relatives know. Please go back to Mr. Berry's store and use his phone. Tell him to put the long distance charges on my bill. Also, call Senator Calhoun's family. Here are the phone numbers. There is so much to do, I hardly know where to begin."

"I'll mow the yard," Billie Joe offered.

"I'll start sweeping," Mary Lou volunteered.

"I'll dust," chimed in Lizzy.

Daisy went into the kitchen. She found Nettie Mae busily working.

"I hope it is okay with you, Ms. Daisy, I went into your garden and picked green beans, corn and tomatoes. I've snapped the beans and shucked the corn. I'll put them into cook if you want me to."

"That would be wonderful. You are so thoughtful."

"I'll make some cornbread. I know this is an awful time for you and the children. Anything to help you, I'm happy to do."

"This is a sad time for all of us. We are used to having Aunt Lillie Fern as part of our lives. It will be a big adjustment."

By evening when it was time to do the chores many neighbors had dropped by, bringing food and some of Adam's young friends had stayed to help. Charlie Jones, the mailman had gotten the word around to everyone on his route. Daisy had often thought as long as Charlie is our mailman, we will not have to have telephones.

When everyone had gone home and the house was quiet, Daisy sat down in her bedroom to think about the events of the day and to plan for the next day. She prayed, asking God to give her the strength to endure, especially for the children, all that would take place in the next two days and all the days to come.

A thunderstorm had come during the night with enough rain to make everything look fresh and green when the Pates got up on Saturday morning. A quiet was over the household instead of the chatter that was usually heard. Each was mourning in their own way in their loss of their dear aunt. They ate their breakfast in silence and went about their farm chores as usual.

Bo, Nettie Mae and their two boys, Samuel and Caleb, came in to help, just as they had done the day before. There were vegetables in the garden that needed picking, butter to be churned and bed linens to be changed to accommodate the relatives that would be coming to spend the night. The parlor needed to be rearranged before Mr. Richardson would be bringing Aunt Lillie Fern's body to lie in state as was the custom.

Uncle Ed and Aunt Myrtle arrived before lunch. Their granddaughter, Lillie Fay, who was named for Aunt Lillie, had driven them. He was the last one living of the siblings of Aunt Lillie Fern. Big tears swelled in his eyes as he hugged Daisy.

"You all have been so good to my sister."

"It was our privilege to have her live with us. We will always miss her." Daisy replied.

After lunch the family members gathered in the parlor to await the arrival of the funeral home, bringing their dear one. It was a sorrowful time for all of them. Mr. Richardson and his helpers carried the casket in and placed it where Daisy directed. After opening it, each person in the room filed by to look upon the sweet face of their dearly departed one. Tears filled their eyes as each one grieved in their own way.

Friends and neighbors came and went during the afternoon. Many of them brought food and vases of flowers. Soon it was time to do the farm chores. Under Bo's direction, everything was taken care of without the Pates having to do anything. The evening meal was served by Nettie Mae and two other ladies. Daisy's thoughts turned to being thankful that they lived in a community of such caring people.

It was a custom for two or three people to sit up all night in the home of the deceased. It was for the respect of the family and to attend to any needs they might have. Calvin and Ida Price had for years appointed themselves as volunteers to do the task. It was a comfort to Daisy to know that they had come for this purpose. A light was left burning all night and with electricity it was an easy thing to do, not like years before when an oil lamp would have been watched to make sure the kerosene did not run out before the night was over. Ellen Smith, who lived alone, stayed to keep them company and to see that the coffee pot was kept warm in case it was needed to keep them awake.

Daisy made sure every one of the city relatives had a place to sleep and was made comfortable. Lizzy and Mary Lou gave up their room and slept with their mother.

Sunday morning dawned without a cloud in the sky. After breakfast, while everyone was still at the dining room table, Uncle Ed said, "Lillie Fern left her will with me with instruction to read it after her death. This will be a good time to take care of it while all of us are together. Most of us will be going back to our homes after the funeral."

They all sat in silence as he continued, "I'll skip the preliminary part about being of sound mind and so forth."

"I bequeath to my niece, Daisy Pate, all my furniture and worldly goods in the house in which I spent my childhood and where I have had the pleasure of living out my last days. I do

not trust the banks with my money these days; I have kept
it in cash in a locked box under my bed. The key is in my
pocketbook in the top drawer of my bureau in my bedroom.
Only Daisy will be the one to open the box. I have already
given my car to her and her children. My insurance policy is
also in the box. Daisy is the beneficiary and will use it to pay
my burial expenses."

Hot tears came into Daisy's eyes. "She thought of everything.
I will not open the box until a few days have passed when my grief
has had some time to settle."

The morning passed and Mr. Richardson came to get the
casket to take it to the meeting house (that is what Quakers refer
to, rather than the name church).

The meeting house was filled to capacity. All the windows were
open and everyone sat fanning with the cardboard fans that had a
picture of Jesus on one side and the advertisement of Richardson's
Funeral Home on the other. When the family had walked into the
meeting house the congregation stood. They walked by the open
casket followed by the congregation, taking the last look at Lilly
Fern before the casket was closed by Mr. Richardson.

The funeral was a beautiful tribute to a person who had lived
a successful, happy and fulfilled life of service to others. Not too
many women in the era in which she lived ever had the opportunity
to live in Washington, D.C. and be the personal secretary of a
senator. Most of those jobs had been filled by men.

After the hymns were sung and the minister preached, Adam
was asked to speak. Choking back tears, he told how his Great
Aunt Lillie Fern had come to live with his family and how much
she had taught and loved them and how much they had appreciated
her and how they would miss her. He sat down and let the tears
flow. Many people were sniffing and wiping their eyes, especially
the women folk.

The people all stood as the funeral home workers pushed the
casket down the aisle, followed by the minister and the six men
pall bearers. The flower girls picked up each wreath and basket of

flowers and walked behind them. Then came the family. Adam walked beside his mother, holding her arm. The congregation followed, all walking in silence to the open grave. The minister read a passage from the Bible and prayed. He then shook hands with each family member, whispering encouraging words to them. The crowd disbursed after many of them greeted the family with hugs and words of sympathy. Some lingered with Daisy and the family, accompanying them back into the meeting house to wait until the burial was completed and the flowers were placed on the grave. They went back to see the grave and to say their last good byes. Uncle Ed had brought his camera and made pictures, promising Daisy he would send her copies.

Bo, Nettie Mae and their two boys had been asked by Daisy to sit with the family at the funeral. After some hesitation they had agreed. In the Quaker tradition, each person, no matter the color of his skin, was equal in the sight of God.

Bo said to Daisy, "We'll be goin' along home now. Don't y'all worry about the evenin' chores; we'll take care of everythin'."

Daisy and the children, along with Uncle Ed and Aunt Myrtle, got into the funeral home limousine to be driven home by Mr. Richardson. Elizabeth and Mary Lou whispered to each other about the enormous automobile. They arrived home. Uncle Ed and Aunt Myrtle said their good byes and left after having a slice of the last pound cake that Lillie Fern had made before her death.

The house was so quiet after everyone was gone. They all went to bed early as it had been a long strenuous day.

On Tuesday night after supper, Daisy decided to open Aunt Lillie Fern's metal box that held her insurance policy and other papers she might need to use to settle her estate. She gathered the children around the dining room table. She opened the box with tears in her eyes.

Inside the box she found envelopes addressed to herself and one for each child. She gave them out. She opened her own first and read it silently to herself. She felt like she was hearing Aunt Lillie Fern's voice.

"My dearest Daisy, thank you for all the happy years I have spent in my childhood home with you and your wonderful family. I have watched them grow during these years into sweet, kind teenagers. You have done a marvelous job of rearing them alone without Joe. After each child has read his letter of what I am bequeathing to each of them, the remainder of my earthly goods belong to you. Thank you for making the last years of my life such a happy time."

"Now each of you can open your envelopes," Daisy smiled through her tears. "You go first, Elizabeth."
She opened her envelope and read aloud,

"My dear Lizzy, I am leaving to you my piano. It has been my pleasure to teach you to play. Also, you and Mary Lou can go through my jewelry box and decide what each of you wants to keep. The $50.00 is for you to start saving toward your college education. I hope that you would want to further your education in music. Love, hugs and kisses, Aunt Lillie Fern."

Lizzy squealed with delight.
Mary Lou opened her envelope.

"My sweet Mary Lou, I leave to you my sewing machine, patterns, books on sewing and my collection of recipe books. You and Lizzy can share my jewelry. The $50.00 is to start your education fund. I am hoping you will want to major in Home Economics and become a teacher. Your skills at sewing and cooking must not be wasted, but should be shared with others. Love, hugs and kisses, Aunt Lillie Fern."

"She knew how much I have enjoyed being in the 4-H Club and now in the Future Homemakers of America. My love for her will be forever."
"Now it is your turn, Billy Joe."
He began to read, choking back tears.

"My dear Billy Joe, because you shared my love for the game of baseball, I leave you my radio so you can listen to all the games as often as you have time. I know someday you will make a name for yourself as the greatest pitcher or catcher or whatever position you choose in all the United States. I hope you will go to college and play on their team before trying for a major league. In whatever you choose to do in life may God bless you and make you successful. Love forever, Aunt Lillie Fern."

"Fifty dollars! I've never had so much money in my whole life, and my very own radio!" Billy Joe exclaimed.

Don't get too carried away. I'm sure she would want you to share your radio with the rest of us," Adam said as he opened his envelope. He read,

"Adam, my special nephew, please open this other envelope enclosed."

He hastened to open it and in it was a receipt from the Admissions Office of the State Agricultural College for tuition, room and board and books for a whole year. Also a note was enclosed that a trust had been set up with the college for three more years if requirements of grades and other rules were met. He jumped up and down, shouting, "Thank you, thank you, Aunt Lillie. Mama, Mama, now I can go to college." He grabbed Daisy, lifting her from the floor and dancing her around in the air. "My dreams are coming true, thanks to Aunt Lillie." The children all jumped up and down with happiness for their brother's good fortune.

After everyone had settled down, Daisy proceeded to look further into the box. There was an envelope with Bo and Nettie Mae's name on it, her insurance policy, the title to her car, her beautiful diamond wedding rings that Senator Calhoun had given her and a diamond necklace that had been his wedding gift. An envelope with several hundred dollars was also there.

When everyone had gone to bed, Daisy sat alone thinking about all that had taken place in the last few days. She breathed a prayer – "Thank you God for all these blessings that you have given us through our dear Aunt."

CHAPTER 16

When college opened in the fall, Adam said his good byes to his family and moved into the dormitory. He had passed all the requirements necessary to start as a freshman. Daisy was sad to see her first born leave home, but happy that Aunt Lillie Fern had made it possible for him to fulfill his dream of going to college.

Billy Joe, Elizabeth and Mary Lou had started back to school. Daisy's crops had flourished and she was able to pay her fertilizer bill and county taxes without going into the money that she had inherited.

There was a war going on in Europe. Adolph Hitler was in power in Germany and everyday the news coming over the radio was very stressful.

The next two years passed quickly, too fast for Daisy as she watched her children grow up. Billy Joe graduated from high school and was recruited by a textile mill to come to work for them and to play on their baseball team. Daisy was disappointed that he did not want to go to college. It was a good opportunity for him, not only to make some money and to have the experience of playing the game he loved. He promised he would go to college later.

Mary Lou and Elizabeth were the only ones left at home. Adam came home every summer to work on the farm and to tell his mother new methods of planting crops that he was learning.

On December 7, 1941, the news came over the radio that Pearl Harbor had been bombed by the Japanese and many of the ships of the United States had been sunk and many lives had been lost. The war in Europe was raging and it wasn't long until the United States was into World War II. Many young men volunteered to go into the service or were drafted. Daisy feared for both her boys.

Billy Joe left his job and joined the Navy. Adam came home from college at the end of his sophomore year. He told his mother that he had something to discuss with her. Daisy dreaded to hear what he had to say.

"Mother, I have been thinking a lot about what I should do ever since I had to register for the draft. I put on my form that I was a 'conscientious objector.' Of course, the man I handed it to raised his eyebrows and asked why. I told him I was a Quaker and I did not believe in war. He said he would put that my religious belief was my reason. He warned me that I would be hearing from the draft board and that I would probably be sent to some place to work that would relieve another man to go into the service. I also told him that I lived on a farm and we raised crops that were necessary to keep the food supply and other necessities."

Daisy replied, "I am proud of you, son. Whatever your conscience tells you is what you must do. One son in the service is enough for me to worry about."

In a few days a letter came informing Adam to report to his local draft board. He went and was told that he was needed to go to work at the State Mental Hospital in Raleigh. He was given a one-way bus ticket and told to be on the bus the following Monday.

"At least I will not be too far from home," he told his mother and sisters at supper that night. I have to take my own clothes and I will not be paid, but I will have room and board. One of my friends is being sent to West Virginia to work in a coal mine."

"I wish you were deferred for farming. I know some men that have been. And too, I wish you could finish your education," Daisy said with a worried look on her face. "I've heard some awful tales of how hard it is to work with mentally ill people."

"Don't worry, mother. I'm strong and can take care of myself. I'll write you a letter every week."

"Will you ever get to come home?" Lizzy asked.

"I'm not sure about that. But you all can come to see me."

"I'll miss you just like I miss Billy Joe."

"Billy Joe might get to come home for a visit after he finished his training and before he is assigned to a ship," Mary Lou said excitedly. "I'm sure he looks good in his uniform."

Daisy sighed, "I wish he could have gotten home before you leave, Adam. Perhaps we can drive over to see you while he is here. I've heard that gas and tires and many other things are going to be rationed. Right away we will be issued ration books that have stamps in them and the merchants will pull them out when we buy things. Sugar is going to be one of the things. I hope I have enough on hand to make blackberry jelly. They are getting ripe along the edge of the pasture behind the barn. Girls, we will have to pick some tomorrow."

"The world is changing so fast," Adam replied. "I hope and pray this war will be over soon and all of us can be together again."

The war continued. Adam found his job to be very difficult. They were short of help and supplies. He worked long hours and tried to remain cheerful as so many of the other workers were almost as depressed as the patients. Daisy had written to the congressman of her district and begged him to see if he could do anything to get Adam deferred to come back to work on the farm. Bo was overworked and outside help was hard to find. Most all of the younger generation had gone into one of he branches of service or had gone to work in the factories that made things for the war effort. The other farmers in the community were facing the same situation.

One day, Charlie Jones, the mailman, blew his horn of his noisy automobile and shouted, "Daisy, you have a letter from Washington. Must be something important!" Instead of putting it in her mailbox, he brought it to her house.

"Well, ain't you going to open it?" Charlie asked.

Daisy didn't answer him and went back into the house.

"I hope it ain't bad news," Charlie shouted as he drove away.

Daisy slowly opened the letter from Congressman White.

"I am happy to inform you that, as you requested, your son, Adam Pate, will be relieved of his job at the State Mental

*Hospital and will be allowed to return to your farm to work
as day labor to raise crops that are useful to feed and clothe
our troops. Please continue to grow as many acres of cotton as
your county allotment allows."*

Daisy jumped up and down, shouting "Hallelujah, thank you
Lord, Adam is coming home. I can't wait until the girls get home
from school. They will be thrilled as I am. He will be here in time
to plant the cotton crop. I'll send him the money for his bus ticket
tomorrow. I would drive over to get him but gas is so scarce and
the tires on Aunt Lillie Fern's car are getting mighty thin and it is
almost impossible to get new ones. The expression 'use it up, wear
it out, make it do, or do without' is really coming true these days."

Adam arrived home the following Saturday.

"It is so good to be back on this farm. I seldom ever got to get
outside and you all know that I am one who loves the land, the
trees, the grass, the sunshine and all that goes with being a farm
boy! I know farming is hard work, but it is nothing compared to
what I have experienced seven days a week this past year. Thank
you, mother, for being persistent in getting me back to farming. It
will be great to be able to attend Meeting on Sundays once again.
I suppose our attendance has dropped off with so many people
leaving the area to work in what we call war plants."

"Yes, our congregation is mainly older folks. Everyone will be
happy to see you."

The cotton crop was planted and the girls worked alongside
their mother to try to keep the grass and weeds hoed out. Mary
Lou graduated from high school and applied to nursing school
for the fall semester. She was accepted at the Catholic Hospital in
Raleigh. It was a known fact that nuns were strict teachers, but
often graduation nurses really were well trained and could get jobs
easier than from some of the other schools. She had met a boy
who had moved to her high school class her junior year. He had
taken her to their senior banquet and they had worked together
on several projects. He had been drafted into the Army right after
graduation. They had promised to write to each other.

She had looked forward to getting his letter. If she was near the mailbox, Charlie Jones would shout, "You got a letter from your sweetheart today!"

Sometimes she would ignore his remark and other times she would say "Thank you for delivering it." Often she would think to her self, "He knows all our business. He is the nosiest person alive, but as mother says, he means well."

The news on the radio was disheartening as the war in both Europe and the South Pacific raged on. Letters from Billy Joe became fewer and far between. Daisy prayed that he would be safe. One evening Gabriel Heater announced on the six o'clock news that a ship had been sunk off the coast of one of the islands that Japan had recently taken over. Only a few of the sailors had made it to shore and were taken captive by the Japanese.

Daisy's heart sank as she heard the news. "Lord, please do not let it be Billy Joe's ship. I know that is a selfish prayer because all those who lost their lives were sons of other mothers."

A few days later a boy on a bicycle delivered a telegram. It read,

> *"This is to inform you hat Billy Joe Pate is listed as missing in action. The ship on which he was assigned has been sunk and only a few survivors escaped and were captured by enemy soldiers. At this time we are unable to know the names of those who were taken captive."*

Daisy collapsed into a chair, sobbing. Mary Lou and Lizzy hugged each other, crying loudly. Adam came into the room and Daisy handed him the telegram. He wept, hugging his mother.

"Mother, we do have the hope that he is among those who got to shore."

"Yes, but being in a Japanese prison camp can be worse than death," she cried. "All we can do is pray for him."

Weeks passed without any other word from the Navy Department.

One day in late August another telegram came informing them that the island where the Navy men had escaped to had been liberated by the U.S. Marines and a person named Billy Joe Pate was among the prisoners found there.

"He's alive, he's alive," screamed Daisy as she rushed to tell the others.

Joy had again come to the Pate household. When they had time to sit down and think about Billy Joe's situation, sadness overwhelmed them. Each person wondered what Billy Joe might have endured at the hands of the enemy. They had heard of the treatment many of the troops had faced, hunger, beatings, denial of water, hard labor and other inhumane treatment.

"All we can do is pray that God has protected him," Daisy told the others.

The next day the news they heard by telegram was that he had been sent to a hospital in San Diego, California. "He is here in the States," Daisy exclaimed as she read the telegram over and over. "I wish I could go see him."

"Mother, why don't you go?" Adam asked. "You can go on the train. I know it is a long trip, but it will give you more peace of mind to see him. You will have to find out more details as to where to go."

"I would like to go, but I have never been on a train in my life. Besides, there is so much to do here on the farm. The cotton will be ready to pick soon."

"Maybe we will get a letter from him," Lizzy chimed in. "Thank you, God, for allowing him to live. Please return him to us soon."

A few days later, while they were eating their lunch after working all morning on the farm, they heard the chug-chug of Charlie Jones' car and he was blowing his horn. They all three ran out to see what all the fuss was about.

"You all got a letter here from the Naval Hospital in San Diego, California. Must be from Billy Joe," Charlie drawled excitingly. Daisy grabbed it and tore it open as Charlie waited to hear the news.

"Dear Mother, I'm here in the Naval Hospital. I know all of you are worried about me. I am getting better everyday.

My main problem when I was found was malnutrition and dehydration. Also, the fingers on my left hand had been broken and healed by themselves. They were crooked and I could not bend them. I have had surgery and I believe they will be as good as new. I'm thankful that it was my left hand and not my right as I can still pitch a baseball. I will be out of the hospital soon and will be coming home by train. I am looking forward to seeing all of you and eating your good cooking again. I love all – Billy Joe."

They were jumping up and hugging each other and Charlie got out of his car and joined them.

"I'm gonna' tell everybody I see that Billy Joe is coming home. Hot diggity, that's the best news I've had to report since Miz Craven's grandson was found alive in France."

The days seemed to drag. Daisy and Lizzy wrote letters to Billy Joe so he would receive one everyday. A telegram finally came instructing them to meet him at the train on September 1, at 2:00 p.m.

"I'll get word to Mary Lou to try to come home and be with us when we go to pick him up," Daisy said as she began to get his old room cleaned up. No one had slept in it since he left home. "I'll cook all his favorite foods, fried chicken and gravy and mashed potatoes and, of course, a pound cake made by Aunt Lillie's recipe."

September 1st finally came. Mary Lou had come home for the weekend and they all went early to meet the train so they would be there when it pulled into the station. Several of the neighbors were there to welcome Billy Joe, including a group of elderly men with instruments who were playing patriotic songs loudly. Charlie Jones was playing a drum. He was dressed in his old uniform from the days he had served in the Navy when he was young. He had always enjoyed telling anyone who would listen how he had run away from home when he was fifteen years old and had lied about his age and joined the Navy. He loved to tell about the time his ship had pulled into port at Singapore and how they were allowed to get off and go into town and mingle with the Chinese people.

"I'm sure Charlie had something to do with organizing this welcome home party for Billy Joe," Adam said. "He's almost as excited as if it were a member of his own family."

When the train came to a stop, the band was playing a World War I tune, "When Johnny Comes Marching Home Again." Daisy and the family rushed to greet Billy Joe. What they saw was not the robust healthy boy, but a very thin, pale man with sunken eyes and cheekbones that stuck out for the lack of fat. His left hand was in a cast up to his elbow and held close to his side by a sling tied around his neck. The smile on his face and the light in his eyes were the same. All Daisy could think about was he was home and she would have to fatten him up.

After all the hugs and kisses and handshakes, Billy Joe said, "Where's the fried chicken, Mom?"

"It's at home waiting for you to eat it," Daisy replied.

"Home, that is the sweetest word I can ever hear. At times I did not think I would see the red clay of North Carolina ever again. But thanks be to God I am here. I can't wait to sleep in my own bed."

"Do you have to report back to the Navy after your hand heals?" Lizzy asked.

"No, I have my discharge paper with me. Mom, I'll be here to help you and Adam on the farm. I can pick cotton with one hand."

"It will be wonderful to have you here."

"When do you graduate from nursing school, Mary Lou?"

"I'll be finished in December and I already have a job in a Veteran's Hospital."

"Do you still write to that guy you met in high school?"

"I surely do. When he gets out of the Army you all just might hear wedding bells ringing."

"It's that serious?" her mother asked.

"It really is. He asked me in a letter and I wrote back with a definite yes."

"I am so happy for you," Lizzy said, hugging her sister. "Am I going to be in the wedding?"

"Of course, I'd like to have you as my maid of honor."

"I'd be delighted."

"Hank Hancock is his name and I can't wait for you boys to meet him. Mother and Lizzy met him when he took me to the junior-senior banquet. He plans to go to college when he gets out."

Billy Joe continued to get his strength back and gradually his muscles filled out. After the cast was removed from his hand, he did physical therapy everyday as he had been instructed. One day he got out his baseball bat and began to swing it. Then he put his baseball glove on and was able to catch balls that Adam threw to him. He seldom talked about his experience as a prisoner of war. Sometimes at night he would awaken shouting, "Please do not hit me again." At first it alarmed Daisy and Adam, but as time went on he was able to sleep soundly without the nightmares.

Daisy noticed he had been writing in a journal. She found it while cleaning his room. Though tempted to read it, she did not want to invade his privacy. Perhaps someday he will allow me to read it, she thought to herself. That day came right at Christmas. He wrapped the journal in paper and placed it under the Christmas tree with her name on it. She unwrapped it on Christmas morning, but did not read it until the holidays were over.

Tears would come to her eyes as she read about the starvation and beating he had endured.

Finally, when I and two other men could take it no longer, we escaped into the jungle. Not knowing where we were going, we kept walking, surviving on nuts and berries, water from streams we found along the way. One day, deep into the jungle, we heard voices. We thought it was the enemy, but looking and listening closer we heard a man speaking English. In a soft voice we heard him reciting from the Bible. I recognized the words from all my years in Sunday school and church and could almost hear my mother reading out loud to me and my brother and two sisters when we had evening devotions before going to bed."

"I whispered to the other two men that this must be a preacher and before our eyes we saw to whom he was reciting. It was a dozen children dressed in ragged clothes, all sitting on the ground. Being afraid we would startle them, I started to sing 'Jesus Loves Me' in a low voice. The man turned to see who was singing as the children scampered away to hide.

"Who is there?" asked the man.

"We are Americans escaped from the Japanese prison camp. We will do you no harm. See, we have no weapons."

"Come closer," he said. The three of us, so dirty and ragged, came closer to him. He reached out his hand and told us his name. He was Herman Roberts, a missionary from Texas. He and his wife, Ruth, had been sent by their church to build an orphanage on this island. They were doing well until the Japanese invaded their village a few months before. He and these children including his own son had escaped into the jungle before the Japanese had gotten to the village. His wife had stayed behind to help some of the elderly to escape, but she had been killed along with those she was trying to help. Thinking they had destroyed everyone in the village and plundered everything they could use, they had moved on out to the next village to do the same.

"The children and I have been living in this cave for weeks. We eat whatever we can find. There is a stream that has fish and we catch them. Once in a while we are able to catch some small animal. There are berries and plants here in the jungle that we eat. I slipped back into the village and gave my wife a Christian burial, along with the others who were with her. I have brought books so I could teach the children and other things to help us survive that the enemy did not destroy. We are afraid to move back to the village for fear of the Japanese coming back. So far, they have never come looking for us. I have a small radio that runs on batteries. I don't use it often to save the batteries, but I try to keep up on the news and pray

everyday that the war will be over. I heard that the war in Europe is over and Hitler is dead.

The other men and I sat down and the children came out of hiding. It was lunchtime and Mr. Roberts shared their meager food with us.

We spent the night with them. The next day we decided what we should do. Mr. Roberts told us that about ten miles due west was a town. It had an airstrip that small planes flew into and was on the ocean that ships came into port, that it was where his wife and son and himself had flown into when they arrived in 1941. "Perhaps there are a few people left there and if the Japanese haven't destroyed it, you might find refuge." After saying a prayer for our safety, he bid us good bye. I will never forget him and those children. He told me the name and gave me the phone number for the church in Texas. When I arrived at the hospital in California, I called the church and spoke to the pastor. I told him that Mr. Roberts and his son and a dozen children were alive, that Mrs. Roberts was dead. He cried when I conferred that they had escaped from the Japanese. He was so happy to hear news of them as it had been months since they had a letter.

We walked in the direction that Mr. Roberts told us. When we got near the town we were hungry and worn out. Mr. Roberts had given us a little money that he said we could use to buy some food. I washed my face and hair in a stream of water and smoothed my hair best I could and left Moore and Phillips waiting outside the town. I kept my eyes open to make sure there were no enemy soldiers on the streets. I did not see any. Mr. Roberts had told me of a store that was run by Christians and had given me instructions as to how to find it.

I went to the back of the store and knocked on the door. Finally a lady and man opened the door. I knew by the look on their faces that they were surprised to see a rag-tag white man standing there. I was not sure that they would understand English. I stuck out my hand to shake the man's hand, stating my name and told them that Herman Roberts had sent me.

117

The moment they heard his name, they asked me to come in. I made them understand that I needed food and showed them the few coins that Mr. Roberts had given me. With hand gestures I made them know that there were three of us. They gathered up three loaves of bread and three jars of something that looked like jelly. They kept saying tea and pointing to the stairs that led to an upper floor. I assumed that it was their living quarters and they were asking me to come have tea with them. I politely shook my head no and tried to make them understand that I had to get back to the other two men. I held out the coins to pay for the food. They both declined. I thanked them and ran out the way I had come in and made my way carefully back to where I had left Moore and Phillips. They had both fallen asleep on the ground. I awakened them and quickly handed them the food. I said a quick blessing, thanking the Lord for our good fortune. Never in my life had I tasted anything so good as that bread and jelly. We each saved a little of it to eat the next day. We sat around wondering what we should do next. I had not seen any Japanese soldiers walking around on the streets. They must not have discovered this small town or thought it wasn't any danger to them. We slept the best that night we had in days.

The next morning we ate the remainder of our food and drank water from a little waterfall at a nearby stream. We had lost track of what month it was and one day had gone into the next. However, I had noticed a calendar on the wall of the market. Even thought I could not read the language, I made out the month as being August 1945. Suddenly we heard what sounded like a marching band and some sort of parade in the town, horns were blowing, people singing and shouting, but we could not understand their language. We ran up to the street where all the noise was coming from. We saw a jeep with U.S. Army on the side of it. The driver saw us and grabbed a bullhorn and the most wonderful sound came over it. "The war is over, the Japanese have surrendered." The three of us began to jump up and down and joined in the shouting. When the parade had gone the length of the town, the jeep came back to us. He inquired what three Americans were doing here. We told him our story and each of us showed him our dog tags that the Japanese had not taken from us. He invited us to get into the jeep and took us to the opposite side of the island from where our ship had sunk and out in the harbor was a ship. We told him about the prison camp that we had escaped from on the other side of the island, and about Mr. Roberts and the children who were hiding in he jungle. He conveyed the message to the officer in charge and soon a convoy was on its way to go to the other side. I volunteered to go with them. Moore and Phillips were sent out to the ship.

It was a very rough ride as there were no paved roads. We really did not know where we were going. Two of the native men were with us and helped with directions. After what seemed almost a day's journey, we came upon a clearing. "This is it," I told the fellow in command. "This is where we were held prisoners." With guns drawn, we made our way into what had been a place with some buildings and straw huts. Everything had been burned to the ground and no sign of life was evident. Tears came to my eyes as I wondered what had happened to the other prisoners. Had they been killed, had they run away into the jungle, or worse, had they been taken by the Japanese by ship to be used as hostages?

We left there and on our way back I tried to determine where Mr. Roberts and the children might be. I spotted a road that looked as if it h ad been traveled and told the driver of the jeep I was in to please go down that road. We followed it and it led to the village and what a wonderful surprise! There was the whole bunch of them. They had come out of the jungle and back to what had once been the building that housed the orphanage. There was much happiness as we pulled into the camp. Mr. Roberts said he had heard on his radio that the Japanese had surrendered and the war was over! He motioned for us to come into the building. There, lying on make-shift beds, were all eight of the other prisoners. My prayers had been answered. They were all thin from lack of food, but every one of them smiled when they saw us. The commander of our convoy shouted for the food and water and medicine that we had with us. Not only the men were fed, but the children also. The commander ordered by radio to get more supplies from the ship. I forgot to say that the ship was a hospital ship equipped with needed supplies for rescuing the wounded and sick.

Mr. Roberts told us that he would like us to take him and the children to the town where there would be food and lodging until he could make contact with the church that was sponsoring him and his work. He told us that the island belonged to the Philippine government and the children could not be taken away without permission. I was wishing I could bring everyone of them home with me! It was sort of hard to tell them good bye as I boarded the ship, but I promised to return some day. And that is how I wound up in the hospital in California. I thank God everyday that He spared my life and I could return to my loved ones. Written by Billy Joe Pate, December 1945.

Daisy kept wiping her eyes all the time she was reading. "My poor child!" she said out loud. "What horrible things have happened to you?" She fell to her knees and thanked God that his life had been spared and that he had been safely returned to her. "It must have been hard for him to write all of this down. I'm glad he did. Now, I understand why he has had those dreams and has awakened screaming. I will let the others read this."

CHAPTER 17

Billie Joe had been accepted for the spring semester at Guilford College. He had decided that he would like to become a high school teacher. His dream of being a baseball player on a major league team had faded away and perhaps he would be able to some day help some other young men fulfill their dreams. Like many others getting out of service to his country, he would be able to take advantage of funds that the government had decided to give to help attain an education. Daisy was happy that he would not be too far away and could come home often on weekends.

Mary Lou's Hank was discharged from the Army, came home and started to college. They dated as often as their busy schedules allowed. On Valentine's day Hank gave Mary Lou a beautiful diamond ring and they began making plans for a June wedding.

One day Adam came home after having been to the new hardware store that had recently been built in Pleasant Grove. He was whistling a tune that Daisy recognized as one that was made popular when he was in high school.

"What are you so happy about?"

"You will never guess who I saw in the hardware store this morning."

"Who?"

"Linda Mae Turner, or that was her name in school. She is back home living with her parents. We talked for about 30 minutes. So much has happened to her since we graduated."

"Let's sit down and eat lunch and you can fill me in."

"She went away to college in Virginia and got a teaching degree. While in school she met a man named Luke Green. He joined the Navy right after graduation. He became a commissioned officer and they got married right after he graduated from officer's training. They were stationed in several different states and in most places she would get a job teaching math in a high school. They were stationed in Seattle, Washington, and Luke was sent on a ship to the Pacific. Of course, she could not go with him so she stayed in Seattle. After he left she found that she was pregnant. She has a beautiful little five-year-old boy named Luke Jr. But, Mother, the sad part is that her husband's ship sank and he never got to see his son. She had a good teaching job and stayed on there. She has moved back here because her parents are getting up in age. Her dad had a stroke and her mother needs her. She is just as pretty as she was when I took her to our senior banquet in 1939. She wanted to hear about my life. I told her that there wasn't much to tell. When I told her that I was not married, she invited me to come have dinner at their house this coming Friday night."

"Adam, slow down. I haven't seen you this excited about anything in such a long time."

"I am excited! You know I never have dated very much. The girls in this community, what few are left, haven't paid much attention to me. One of them told me she didn't want to marry a farmer, that she had enough farm life growing up."

Friday afternoon came and Adam went to get a haircut at Willie's Barber Shop in Pleasant Grove. He had to wait a few minutes and Charlie Jones came in to wait his time.

Charlie, being as nosey as ever, said, "Adam, you must have a date tonight, getting your haircut on Friday afternoon. That's somethin' you usually do on Saturday afternoon."

Adam ignored his remark.

"I hear tell that Linda Mae Turner has come home to help out her folks. Didn't you used to be sweet on her when y'all were in high school? She's a widow with a little boy and you two would make a fine couple."

"Now, Charlie, what makes you think that?"

"I saw you talkin' to her in the hardware store the other day. Now that I'm retired from my mail carryin' job, I have more time to sit around and jaw with my man friends."

Willie spoke up, "Charlie, you sure do and you know everybody's business in this whole county. I heard somebody say one time that none of us needed a telephone as long as Charlie Jones is livin'. By the way, I heard that the Bell Telephone Company is planning to start puttin' up poles and stringin' phone wires all the way from Raleigh to Pleasant Grove. I'll probably have more business when we all have phones. Might even have to buy me another barber chair and hire another barber."

As Adam climbed into the barber chair he said to Charlie, "We do miss you, Charlie. You always kept us informed as to what was going on in the community. The new person is a lady, and I guess we have to call her the mailwoman. She doesn't take time to chat with us like you always did."

"Thank you, Adam. That makes me feel like somebody 'preciated me. How's the rest of your family?"

"All doing well. Did you know we have hired another man to help us? He's a friend of Bo's. Works as a day laborer. Goes home to his family every night. It has helped us so much. My mother doesn't have to work so hard now."

"That Daisy Pate is the workingest woman I have ever known. She sure has done a fine job raisin' you four younguns by herself. When she came back to her granddaddy's farm I didn't think she could ever make a go of it by herself. But she did and she has a right to be proud of herself."

"If Bo had not come along and been willing to stay and help us, I don't know if she could have made it. She calls him a gift from God."

Willie nodded his head yes and Charlie agreed.

Adam went to the Turner house for dinner. Like her mother, Linda was a good cook. He was introduced to Luke Jr.

The first thing Luke said was, "Do you have any horses?"

Adam replied, "No, but we have two mules and a tractor."

"I like horses. Mommy said we might get one now that we are living here with grandma and grandpa." "That sounds like a good idea. Maybe you would like to start off with a pony."

"Do you know anyone that has a pony?"

"Well, I can't think of anyone right now, but I'm sure there are some ponies on some of the farms around here."

"Mommy, could we get a pony?"

"We will see about it, Luke."

He ran to his grandfather, who was sitting in his wheel chair. "Grandpa, Mommy said we might get me a pony. Don't you think we could keep it in your barn?"

Mr. Turner smiled and said, "That's a good idea."

The evening passed quickly as Adam and Linda sat talking about their school days. Adam said, "It's ten o'clock. We farmers have to get up early. I better get on home. I've really enjoyed the dinner and our conversation and, of course, meeting Luke."

When he got home everyone had gone to bed. He mused to himself that he was glad that he didn't have to answer questions about his evening.

Lizzy graduated from high school in June, with honors, and was the first Pate child to have to go twelve years to school. North Carolina had changed graduation from eleven grades to twelve. She was excited about attending college in the fall. But the most exciting thing in the Pate household was the upcoming wedding of Mary Lou and Hank.

Daisy and Lizzy had done much of the work of getting the wedding plans made since Mary Lou was working. Hank was gong to summer school, so the wedding had to be squeezed in between the spring semester and summer school. Hank had decided that he would like to become a medical doctor. That meant several years of school. All the Pates had agreed that having a doctor and a nurse in the family would really be a great asset.

The wedding was held on a beautiful Saturday afternoon in early June in the Quaker Meeting House. Mary Lou was escorted down the aisle by Adam who was giving her away. She wore Daisy's wedding dress that had been carefully preserved for this occasion. Billy Joe was the best man. Lizzy wore a peach-colored dress as maid of honor, one that she had designed and made with the help of her mother. An outdoor reception was held on the lawn at the Pate home. Most all the members of the church and community turned out for the joyous occasion. The happy couple left for a short honeymoon at Carolina Beach.

Later that week Daisy sat on the front porch snapping the first green beans that she had picked from the garden. To have fresh vegetables to eat and to feed her family had always been one of her many blessings that she truly appreciated.

No one was around, only the buzzing of the bees and the singing of the birds made the solitude of the moment precious to Daisy. She had time to think back over her life. She appreciated these times when she could talk to Joe as if he was sitting beside her.

"My dear Joe, I still miss you. I do wish you could have been here to see our children grow up. We've got one happily married and three more to go. Adam is the happiest I've seen him in a long time ever since he has found Linda Mae again. I always thought that he was in love with her in high school. He never said it out loud, but I could tell he was disappointed when she went off to college and never wrote to him. Even when she came home for holidays she never contacted him. He was too bashful and too busy with his life here on the farm to make an effort to see her. Now, he is talking about building a house and has picked out the spot for it. Her father has died and her mother wants to give up their farm and move into one of those places they are building for older folks to live out their years in. She feels she is holding Linda back from living the life that she should have and giving little Luke the father figure he needs. Linda has gone back to teaching school now that Luke is in school.

As to Billy Joe, he is dong well in college, is home to help us this summer. He brought a very nice lady who has already finished college to Mary Lou's wedding. I was very impressed with her. I guess I am selfish, but when he gets his teaching degree, I hope he will find a high school near here so I can see him often.

Lizzy is thinking of a career in being a fashion designer. Since the war, companies are building textile mills all over the South and giving many people jobs. Her dream is to create designs for making fabric as well as designing clothes to be made from it.

That is why she is going to the State University. Not too many women are allowed into that field. She is thrilled that she has been accepted. She said if she couldn't make it there, she could always teach home economics in a school somewhere. Some folks say she is just like me, always trying to do something that not everyone would attempt.

When I look back to the year I was left alone with four children to raise on this farm without a dime to my name and you only with me in spirit, Joe, without determination I would never have made it. I saw other women lose their children whose husbands had died or some whose men had run off and left them when the hard times of the great depression in his country sucked the life out of ways to make a living. Many were sent to orphanages or placed in foster homes or even put in what was known as "work houses." I was determined that no one would ever take my children from me. The good Lord blessed me and allowed me to inherit this farm and I knew that we could at least raise food to eat and would have a roof over our heads. It was a struggle to pay the taxes and to send the children to school. Without Aunt Lillie Fern coming to live with us I might have thrown up my hands and called it quits! I feel like God sent Bo to help us. Without him I would not have been able to plant the crops and harvest them. I am so thankful that I was able to rear our children here instead of in a city where there are so many temptations. Now that World War II is over, I am looking forward to spending my old age right here. This house is going to eventually be mighty big for just me, but hopefully one day it will be filled with grandchildren playing and having as much fun and laughter as our children had. We already have a good start with Luke coming over with Adam and Linda Mae. Joe, I do wish you could have been with us on this journey, but I know you are in a better place.

Daisy was startled when Lizzy came out on the porch. "Mother, have you finished stringing those beans?" I need to get them on to cook. There will be two hungry men coming in to eat their supper before the beans are done."

"Oh! I guess I have been sitting here daydreaming. I was thinking about our lives and how we have lived through the depression days and World War II and have come a long way without giving up."

"With a mother like you to guide us and protect us, that thought never crossed our minds."

"I was thinking about your father and how proud he would be of each of you. He was a wonderful man, full of life and looking forward to helping me rear the four of you. Who knows, if he had lived we might have had more children. I always thought it would have been wonderful to have twins. But God in his infinite wisdom had other plans."

"I was so little when he died that I cannot remember too much about him. But I know he must have been very special, knowing you, or you would not have married him. I love to look at your wedding picture and all the other pictures we have of him. I used to dream of him holding me in his arms like in one of the pictures."

"He really loved me and all his children. It is so comforting to remember that."

"Let's get these beans on to cook. Mother, you ought to write a book about all your experiences of raising four children all by yourself. You always have had so much hope for all of us. You could name your book, *Daisy's Hope for her Journey*."

She gave her mother a big hug and the bowl of green beans overturned onto the porch floor. They both roared with laughter as they scrambled to pick them up.

"Just look who spilled the beans this time!" Daisy said.